"Pull up there, driver! Or you're a dead man!"

Almost in the same instant a rifle barrel poked through the window of the stage. "Everybody out and hands up! High!"

Climbing down, Clint Adams saw four men. He heard the driver telling them, "There ain't no money aboard today. There's nothing but a mail sack for Virginia City."

"I take it you boys are after loot," Clint said. He bent down, though not too swiftly, and let his hand reach his boot.

"Real easy like!" The bandit chief was pointing his Colt right at Clint's head.

Kneeling down, the Gunsmith pulled off his boot, took out the folded bills, and pulled his boot back on. One of the bandits whistled. "Looks like good solid scrip."

"Couple of thousand there," the Gunsmith said, starting to get up, "and more where that came from." He tossed the money easily at the tall man, and for a moment the bandits were distracted.

In that flashing moment, Clint pulled out the knife he'd had strapped to his leg, and in one fluid motion whipped it right into the man with the gun . . . .

Don't miss any of the lusty, hard-riding action
in the Charter Western series, THE GUNSMITH

And coming next month:
THE GUNSMITH #62: BOOM TOWN KILLER

THE GUNSMITH

61

THE COMSTOCK GOLD FRAUD

J. R. ROBERTS

CHARTER BOOKS, NEW YORK

THE GUNSMITH #61: THE COMSTOCK GOLD FRAUD

A Charter Book / published by arrangement with
the author

PRINTING HISTORY
Charter edition / January 1987

ISBN: 0-441-30965-8

Charter Books are published by The Berkley Publishing Group,
200 Madison Avenue, New York, New York 10016.
PRINTED IN THE UNITED STATES OF AMERICA

ONE

The big man at Elk Lodge hadn't been easy. He'd even pulled a knife—after Clint Adams had dropped him and kicked his big hogleg well out of reach—and had come slashing at his opponent's crotch. The tip of the big buffalo knife had just nicked Clint on the front of his thigh. Close, and scary; and so he'd finished the big man off with a tremendous kick right into his Adam's apple.

That hadn't ended the matter, but had created a useful pause.

"You know that feller?" Clint had his back to the bar, and the sour voice came from behind him.

"Don't know and don't care," the Gunsmith said, turning to face the skinny man on the sober side of the bar. He lifted his glass of whiskey. "At least he didn't spill my drink," he observed wryly. He looked back down at the still prone giant, who was having trouble breathing.

"You have just coldcocked the owner of this here establishment, and one of the big men in town to boot," the bartender said. "And by the way, the cute

1

little cause of this here fracas happens to be his girl-friend, stranger."

Clint grinned as he leaned on the bar and looked at the little redhead with the big, bouncy bust. She was climbing to the upstairs rooms. Well, he hadn't known that, and even if he had, so what? The girl had offered it to him for free, and he'd been turning it over when the big sonofabitch with hands like mallets had suddenly grabbed him.

"And if I was you, mister, I would be mighty careful," the stringy man behind the bar went on in his dull, but informative voice. "Big William there don't only fight with his fists." As he said this he lowered his voice considerably.

The merchandise at the Friendly Times Drinking and Gaming Establishment wasn't put out for free, but the Gunsmith had always considered himself an exception to the rule, and he surely intended to stay that way. Looking up at the girl on the balcony now, he grinned back at her as she beckoned with her eyes, her shoulders, and with her very attractive breasts.

Only the onlookers, who instantly made a large space for the short battle and by now had returned to drinking, playing cards, and checking the girls, were also watching warily as the big man lying on the floor began to stir.

"Just a friendly warning," the bartender said, leaning forward and wiping the bar. "I happen to know who you are, Gunsmith."

Clint Adams looked directly at the man now.

"You do, eh . . ."

"And Big William did too. That was no accidental meeting."

The man on the floor started to curse. The Gunsmith had come to a decision. "I appreciate it, mister," he said, and with a flick of his glance at the thin man, turned and went swiftly out of the Friendly Times Drinking and Gaming Establishment.

The Gunsmith had already bought his ticket for the stage to Virginia City, and as he threw his war bag up onto the baggage rack, he spotted a cute little brunette with brown eyes and a figure under a soft dress that suggested a whole lot more than it revealed. He felt his blood race.

Inside the coach, as the driver laid into his whip rounding out of the little town, he let himself fall against his fellow passenger, who moved abruptly away from him.

"Sorry ma'am—uh, miss . . ." Straightening, he touched the brim of his hat in apology.

The grim preacher-looking man sitting opposite scowled from under his bushy eyebrows, and reaching up, settled his stern black stovepipe hat farther down on his forehead.

The girl had moved into the other corner of the seat—she wasn't having any. It could be because he looked a mess, with a bruise on his left cheek, a cut under his right eye, and with the knuckles of his left hand discolored and swollen.

The Gunsmith decided to draw back, too, pulling himself into his corner of the swaying coach. While appearing to doze with the brim of his Stetson hat pulled down over his face, he studied his fellow passengers.

The girl took most of his attention at first. There was about her a rich animal liveliness. Yet she was at the same time contained, not throwing her attractiveness around the coach. He thought she smelled subtly of pine. He found her tantalizing, and smiled to himself under his wide hat brim in anticipation of getting to know her.

Meanwhile he was giving attention to the severe guardian of rectitude and moral deliverance who was sitting opposite, alone on the bench.

The man was stringy, like jerked leather; all bone and hair, with skin stretched tight over his face and hands like the hide on a set of horse panniers. Across the hard tube of his chest a heavy watch chain of dull gold lay against the black broadcloth waistcoat, as though guarding its owner. A drooping mustache framed what was obviously a tight-lipped mouth, and shaggy eyebrows lidded his deep-socketed obsidian eyes.

Clint had decided that the man was an undertaker, or a man of the cloth. Or—the thought sprang into him swiftly—a killer. That suggestion almost made him sit up, but he remained as he was, falling into a doze from the rhythm of the swaying coach.

"Hyah! Hyah!" Clint heard the long whip crack out like a rifle shot as he opened his eyes. The braces creaked as the sweating teams lunged ahead, jerking the coach and rocking the passengers as they charged down into the thin canyon. Dust rose in blinding clouds all around them, and the man in black broadcloth moved to the window to close out the disturbance. Clint noted that his lips were moving silently, and he wondered if the man of God was saying a prayer while the iron tires of the coach rang noisily against the rocky road.

TWO

The stage slowed and began ascending a long grade. The horses were sweating and blowing, for though the stage wasn't heavily laden, the driver had kept the team going at a brisk pace.

At that moment the Gunsmith knew something was wrong. He sensed it with the same instinct that had saved him more than a few times in his life. The thought had hardly touched him when the shot rang out, followed instantly by the voice, hard as a rifle barrel.

"Pull up there, driver! Or you're a dead man!"

The driver, sawing at his reins, brought the team to a halt in a cloud of dust and sweat.

Almost in the same instant a rifle barrel poked through the window of the coach and a voice said, "Everybody out and hands up! High!"

Climbing down, Clint saw four men, though he knew there could have been more backing them out of sight.

"Throw down that sack with the money in it and nobody gets hurt!" It was the first speaker, a tall man high in the chest and shoulders, sitting a tough little bay gelding.

"There ain't no money aboard today," the driver said, standing by his team with his hands raised. "There's nothing but the mail sack for Virginia City." He was a squarely built man in his late thirties. "Why, there ain't even nobody riding shotgun," he added.

"Cut the stalling," snapped the bandit, his voice muffled through a bandanna which covered his face from just below his eyes.

The Gunsmith was glad to see that the four men were masked. There was a chance they weren't planning to kill them then.

The terrified driver had no choice but to insist. "A sack of money was scheduled to come up today," he explained. "But for some reason they didn't put it aboard."

The three passengers had been lined up just beside the stagecoach, by one of the gunmen. The tall man signaled with his handgun for the driver to move over beside them, then nodded to one of his companions, who stepped forward, took their guns, and searched them. Only the Gunsmith and the stage driver were armed.

The total collection came to just under five hundred dollars, the preacher's gold watch and chain, and a diamond ring belonging to the girl. Not much of a haul, and it was plain to see that the bandits were annoyed. Not a good sign, the Gunsmith realized. They could just decide to shoot them out of anger at not finding the big haul they'd been expecting.

The four bandits were standing close to their captives, with the leader closest; he had his eyes on the girl. There was no doubt in Clint Adams's mind what he was thinking.

Suddenly one of the other bandits started forward. "She don't have nothin'," he said. His voice was muffled by his bandanna; a good deal more muffled than necessary, was the thought that crossed the Gunsmith's mind. He was evidently trying also to disguise his voice. "Jake searched her," he said.

"Shut up, you fool!" snapped the leader, his voice cracking like a whip. "Didn't I tell you no names!"

The Gunsmith was watching the girl, who stared at the man with the muffled voice. She dropped her eyes and seemed to draw back.

"Search the stage!" the leader said. "I want to make sure."

The three men went to it quickly, rifling the mail pouch of its contents, coming up with eighteen dollars. Then, following their leader's orders, they unhitched the horses and started them down the road toward Virginia City.

Clint Adams had decided not to try anything with the bandits. They hadn't found his money, which was inside one of his boots. He'd kept some in his pocket, and this he'd given them easily. It was only a few dollars. But he had no intention of parting with the one thousand dollars and the letter from Wells, Fargo contracting his services. The thousand he'd won fair and square at the faro game at the Owl Hoot Saloon at Elk Lodge. Usually he didn't mind parting with money, but he did now. And giving it to a bunch of dirty-looking road agents wasn't his idea of how to spend it.

The young bandit who had drawn the leader's anger by mentioning somebody's name spoke in a low voice to the thin man.

"I know it!" the leader snapped, straightening hard and staring right at the Gunsmith. He'd been chewing vigorously on a cud of tobacco, and now his jaws slowed. He spat a stream of brown and yellow juice at a clump of sage. He had holstered his six-gun and now his hand dropped onto the gun butt while with his other hand he reached up and made sure his mask was well fixed over his face.

Out of the side of his eye Clint caught the girl staring intently at the young bandit again, but then all his attention swept back to the men facing him.

"We better take him along," one of the other bandits said, and the four began to converge on the Gunsmith.

Clint felt the wild look the girl suddenly threw in his direction—a look of surprise and agitation. She had no idea what was going on. The preacher man, on the other hand, hadn't moved a muscle.

"You boys don't search very thoroughly, do you?" the Gunsmith said suddenly.

The appeal to greed worked, the tall leader hesitating.

"What's that mean?" he asked.

"I thought you boys were after loot."

"Big William will want him in one piece," one of the men said.

"Might have to give him a going over, even so," said another, who had not yet spoken.

"I mean, you didn't have your boys search very well," the Gunsmith was saying, his eyes on them like a panther watching for an opening.

Suddenly he bent down, though not too swiftly, and let his hand reach to his boot.

"Hold that!"

"Just reaching to my boot," he said.

The tall man had his six-gun pointing right at the Gunsmith. "You make one more move and you're dead."

"I could tell you where there is loot," Clint Adams said.

"In your boot?"

"Maybe. You got to let us go for me to tell."

"We'll find it," one of the men said.

"I don't have the money with me, but I can show you where it's cached."

"You got a map or somethin'?"

"Just let me get it."

"Get it. But easy like!" The bandit chief was pointing his Colt right at the Gunsmith's head.

Kneeling down, the Gunsmith pulled off his boot, took out the folded bills, and pulled his boot back on.

"Jesus," one of the bandits said. "Looks like good solid scrip."

"Couple of thousand there," the Gunsmith said, starting to get up, "and more where that came from." Suddenly he tossed the packet of money at the tall bandit, easy and friendly: It did the trick—for a split second the man was distracted.

In that flashing moment, he'd pulled up his trouser leg, drawn the long, perfectly balanced and razor-sharp knife from where it had been strapped to his leg, and in one flowing motion zapped it right at the man with the gun.

It was an endless moment as he saw the other bandits reaching for their weapons, the surprise on the tall bandit's face, his scream as the knife blade sank into his leg while the gun he was holding exploded, its bullet racing to nowhere.

Almost before the Colt hit the ground the Gunsmith had it in his hand and was pulling the trigger. The tall man was falling to the ground, holding his thigh, and a second bandit was down, with a bullet in his shoulder. Another had run for cover, and the young bandit who had spoken somebody's name was up on his horse and cutting out. The Gunsmith fired a shot after him, but didn't repeat, for he saw he'd only empty his gun and be facing the remaining bandits with a useless weapon.

"Git on and get out!" he snapped at them. "Take him with you," he added with a nod at the fallen road agent. "He might make it to a doc."

"God Almighty," one of the bandits said with awe. "Man moves like a cat jumpin' off a firecracker!"

"Git!" The Gunsmith had retrieved his gun and gun belt. He was buckling with one hand while holding the three men in his sights with the Colt in his other hand.

In seconds they were gone.

"By God," said the stage driver. "By God, if I hadn't seen it, I wouldn't of believed it. You know who them were?"

"Don't have a notion," Clint said. "But I do know they ain't what they used to be, or whatever they thought they were."

"That was Stash Hammond, the tall one. Don't know the others, but they're likely part of his gang, the Hammond gang."

"I would figure that too," the Gunsmith said wryly, but the stage driver didn't catch his cold humor. "What say we catch them horses and get rolling."

The stage driver had almost returned to normal. He was chewing a fresh cut of tobacco as he came in with the team of horses. They hadn't gone far.

"We'll cut along right quick," he said, and spat onto one of the team's singletrees. "Those fellers will be reporting back to Big William, I have a notion. And it looks to me, mister, that you be going to have yer hands full."

"That is for sure," cut in the preacher. He hadn't said a word since the time the stage had been stopped, but now he began to unbend. "Nice gun work there. I appreciate your getting us out of a tight spot, and I also appreciate how in so doing you ran the risk of getting us all cut off at the pockets, including our young lady here."

"Not a chance," the Gunsmith said. "Anyone that good looking has got to be leading a charmed life." And he was pleased to see the girl flush as she looked away. He had said it for her ears.

"Good enough," the preacher said, and started toward the coach.

"You're interested in how I got us all out of that spot," the Gunsmith said, speaking louder.

The preacher stopped and turned as he was about to climb into the coach. He stood facing back, his eyes on the Gunsmith. The girl had also stopped, hearing something extra in Clint Adams's voice.

"That is correct," the preacher said.

There was a tight grin on the Gunsmith's face as he said, "And I got something interesting me."

"And what could that be?"

It was a charged moment. The girl was watching the two men closely, and even the stage driver had turned his attention to the tableau.

"It could be that gun you're packing under your armpit, and not only why you didn't use it, but why those bandits didn't collect it from you."

"Gun?" The preacher's face had darkened to a very deep red.

Clint Adams watched his fingers twitch.

"Yes—the hideout there."

"Could be my Bible, mister."

"Excepting it is a derringer. And you're no preacher."

"Never said I was."

"True. But I've a notion you're an undertaker, though not the kind that normally follows the profession."

Without waiting for any reply the Gunsmith picked up his scattered money, walked to the far side of the coach, and opening the door, climbed inside. In another moment or two they were on their way, with the Gunsmith keeping his eyes tight on the man wearing the big black stovepipe hat.

THREE

The Gunsmith had never encountered such noisy bedsprings, not in all the occasions when he'd bedded women. The bed at the Boston House screamed and twanged, bumped and thumped, whined and whinnied, and nearly fell apart under the raging excitement of the Gunsmith and the marvelously willing blonde. They were making sounds illustrating their unbelievably exquisite pleasure.

"Oh, my God, come, come! Give it to me!" She was almost shouting it, her lips pressed to his ear as he drove into her and her legs wrapped tight around him as her buttocks pounded in perfect rhythm with his.

Clint Adams had no intention whatever of coming at that moment. He was holding off for as long as he could, teasing out the exquisite agony and pleasure as she squirmed, digging her fingers into his thrashing buttocks. Without even a pause to shift position while the rhythm mounted as they raced to the pinnacle, he squirted his whole load into her and her buttocks slowed as she cried out.

Finally, after what seemed a long time, he felt her

breath in his ear. "Clint, you're wonderful."

"Ginger, you're not too shabby yourself," he said as his organ began to grow right into her again.

This time he rode her more slowly, and she responded in perfect rhythm, her buttocks wiggling, squirming, dancing as he worked his cock up high and deep into her and drove the very breath out of her. They came in a Niagara of come, even more than the first time.

After a while he rolled off her and they lay together in the wide, now at last silent bed, and listened to someone in the room below hammering on the ceiling for quiet.

Half asleep, he lay on his back thinking not of the girl beside him, but of the girl on the Virginia City coach. On their way in she had introduced herself.

"I'm Sally Miller," she'd said simply. "And I want to thank you for getting us out of that mess. Saving our lives."

"My name's Clint Adams," he'd told her, looking right into the scowling visage of the man opposite him. "And what is your monicker, mister?"

"Just call me Starch."

The Gunsmith looked at him appraisingly for a moment. "You know something—that name fits you."

"You trying to be funny?"

"You looking for trouble?"

The man who gave his name as Starch said nothing further, he simply looked away. Clint grinned at the girl.

"You going to be in Virginia City long?"

"I don't know. I have some business." And she looked away, ending the conversation.

At the stage depot he'd tipped his hat to her after helping her down with her baggage. "I'll likely be at the Boston House, miss, if you feel the need for help in any way; or just . . . company," he finished with a grin.

She didn't grin back or even smile. "Thank you, Mr. Adams." She looked quickly over her shoulder, then back at him. "I might . . . I might call on you. I . . . I'm trying to find someone. But . . . well . . ." And with a shy little nod and a flush of embarrassment, she turned away.

Walking down the street toward the Boston House, Clint Adams discovered that he had one of the biggest erections of his life straining wildly against his trousers. Nor had his organ subsided by the time he'd reached his room, taken off his boots, and caught the knock at his door.

Was it her? he'd wondered. He hoped so. What luck! But it was the blonde—the luscious creature now lying naked beside him in his bed as his thoughts wandered dreamily over the past hour or so.

As he'd faced her at the door with his hand within easy reach of the gun at his hip, he'd realized he was still partially erect from his thoughts of Sally Miller. When the cute thing in the doorway asked if she could come in, his member hardened and he had no trouble at all in transferring its allegiance to this new attraction.

The blonde had dropped her eyes to his trousers. "Is that how you always greet strangers, sir?"

"You'll have to ask my friend here," the Gunsmith had replied easily. "Let him speak for himself."

She had moved toward him, but he quickly stepped

around her and locked the door. Then he checked the window.

"Suspicious of something?"

"Just being careful, honey. What can I do for you?"

"I'd like to meet your friend there," she said. She was tall, with a wide mouth, green sleepy-looking eyes, and a pair of breasts that were obviously fighting against her silk dress to be let out, the nipples obviously hard. The Gunsmith felt his breath catching while his organ was almost ripping his pants.

"I'm all for that, honey. But I'm also all for living and not getting beaten up or shot up while I'm having some fun with the establishment's merchandise. You get me?"

She flushed at that. "You get right to the point, don't you."

"Saves time. Tell me who you are and what you want." He looked quickly toward the locked door.

"There's nobody outside. It's not a setup. I work for Hercules Rowayton. You've likely heard of him."

"Yeah! That the same Hercules that had to shovel all that shit out of some stable?"

Her laughter came out like tinkling glass, and drove his erection into a new phase, where he thought he was getting ready to come.

"I'm the welcoming committee. Mr. Rowayton wants to see you."

"Knew I was coming, huh."

"Mr. Rowayton knows just about everything. Like I said, he seems to know your tastes. Why he sent me along." And the eyes that had looked out at him as she stood there with her hands at her sides were as innocent as a young virgin's.

The Gunsmith was inside her before either of them were fully undressed and even before she was lying down. They had finished their undressing while pumping furiously together.

And now, some time later, with the bed about ready to give up, he felt himself exquisitely tired and ready for sleep. Was it three times they'd done it? Or four?

It didn't matter. It certainly didn't matter at all as she reached over and began caressing him into a new rigidity, helping her fingers along by taking him into her mouth and sucking.

FOUR

If Hercules Rowayton knew anything at all about Virginia City, it was simply this: that the town was never the same from one week to the next, from day to day. He loved it.

It was a raw, raucous place, the town's main thoroughfare stretching out in two jumbled lines of shacks leaning crazily against other shacks. Always, along the teetering planks that passed for sidewalks, moved a motley throng: miners, sharpsters, and women whose paint, flouncing hips, and tawdry finery spoke graphically of their profession.

He stood now at the corner of C Street, a big man, square-shouldered, square-handed, hard as the lumber that was being shipped in from the mill to put up the new buildings, a man in his early forties. Handsome, people put it in describing him, until that hard look came into his eyes; and charming until he saw what he considered another's unsuitable behavior. Hercules Rowayton accepted only total fealty from his associates, business or otherwise.

He'd been watching as the coach came in with news of the abortive holdup. Even though he was

19

some distance away, he could tell something was amiss; there was that excitement in the atmosphere which seemed always to spread like the prelude to a storm. It was in the horses, in the driver's body, in the very air the stage brought with it. He saw the girl descend, he saw the Gunsmith, and he saw the man in the black stovepipe hat.

"That him?" asked the voice at his elbow. "That him, Mr. Rowayton?"

Hercules didn't turn, but he duly noted the man's correcting himself in the way he had addressed his employer. Wagner. Wagner had to be reined down once in a while. Hercules Rowayton showed his awareness of the near lapse on the part of his subordinate by not answering him.

Then he spun around. "I want to know what happened. Goddamn it! Somebody fucked it up!"

After a pause Rowayton said, "Get Farkas and Nolan. I want to know Adams's every move."

"Do you want them here, Mr. Rowayton, or at your office?"

"The office, for Christ sake." He turned angrily on the other man, a man smaller than himself, with a thin mustache on his weak lip. A pair of cruel eyes, however, made up for any possible weakness in the rest of Dutch Wagner's appearance. Hercules Rowayton knew how to pick his men. But he was furious at the present incompetence. After all, he had Big William set up at Elk Lodge to keep him informed—which he had in the present instance—but here, Hammond's men had buggered it.

"And send Ginger Keely to me," he said softly, not looking at the other, his eyes on the street where the three passengers had alighted from the stage.

He remained where he was, his eyes still on the scene before him, for the moment leaving his thoughts of the Gunsmith. He loved it. By God, it was the Comstock! And what more could a man ask! As far as he could see from where he stood at the top of C Street, it was one long, endless line of prairie schooners, great wagons filled with ore, huge drays, stagecoaches, and wagons loaded with logs for the timbers and steam engines in the mines. The long wagons were drawn by twenty-mule teams, and behind were three, maybe four more wagons called back-action trailers, loaded with cordwood. These caravans were monstrously long and required the craft, ingenuity, and bull-headedness of drivers who were as tough and relentless as the wild, implacable West itself. It was said that when a man could skin a twenty-mule team through to the Comstock, he didn't need to know anything else. That's all there was.

Remembering this bit of sagacity, Hercules Rowayton shoved his hands into his pockets and started along the street to his office. Where Stash Hammond had failed, maybe Ginger could succeed. Now a fresh thought had started up in his fertile mind—perhaps it might be better not to kill Adams. If he really was being sent for by Wells, Fargo—as he had been informed—why incur the unnecessary attention of the company? And moreover, he was well aware of the Gunsmith's reputation. Maybe something could be worked out. Every man had his price, after all.

He was whistling a soft ditty through his pursed lips as his pace quickened.

FIVE

It was close to evening when the girl reminded him that Hercules Rowayton wanted to see him.

"And you're his invitation card?" he asked as he watched her getting dressed.

She smiled ruefully then. "I'm . . . I'm his." And then she added, looking at the naked Gunsmith sitting on the edge of the ancient bed, "Except sometimes."

"Got'cha."

"I think he'd like to see you right away," she said as she finished dressing and saw that he'd made no move to get up and put on his clothes.

"Tell him I'll turn it over. I've got a pretty full social load right now."

She had her hand on the doorknob. "I don't know if you know who Mr. Rowayton is, but it's a good notion to do what he asks."

Later, as he came downstairs, he wondered about the events of the past few hours. The bandits had mentioned Big William, the giant he had beaten back at Elk Lodge; that was point number one. Number two, Mr. Hercules Rowayton had somehow been expecting him, and clearly he wasn't working for Wells, Fargo. How did Rowayton know he was here, or even know who he was? Not that the Gunsmith's reputation was hiding under a bushel. He was certainly known, a fact he considered a devastating shame, and indeed he did all he could to lessen any notoriety attached to his name. But it was a fact of life—people wanted heroes and villains, they wanted drama. And right now three people—at least three— wanted the Gunsmith: Wells, Fargo; Big William; and Hercules Rowayton. He wondered if Big William and Rowayton might be connected. He, on the other hand, wanted Miss Sally Miller.

To his astonishment there was a message for him at the desk when he got downstairs. The girl was waiting for him in the dining room. He spotted her the moment he entered. She was at a table in the far corner, with a cup of coffee and an open book in front of her.

"Interesting?" he asked as she looked up at his approach.

Her expression was neutral as she closed her book. "I think so. It's about a whale."

He sat down opposite her, taking off his hat and placing it carefully on a nearby chair.

"What can I do for you, Miss Miller?" He turned his full attention to the widely spaced brown eyes, the full lips, the delightful bit of an ear peering out from under the dark brown hair; not to mention the full, young, and springy bosom that pushed into the table in front of her. She had small, delicate, yet strong hands. He wanted to take one, turn it over, look at her palm, and feel it.

"I want to ask you something." She had moved

her coffee cup and book out of the way, and now, leaning forward a little, she folded her hands together on the table. "I want you to find my brothers." She was looking straight at him as she spoke, and he could see she was controlling herself.

"Tell me more."

She looked down at her hands. "There isn't a whole lot to tell. Tom and Dave, I'm the middle one, left home—home is Ohio—three years ago to come out west and . . . well I don't know what; maybe they were looking for adventure. Anyway, Tom's the oldest and he left first, then it seems he sent for Dave. Well, they used to write, and then suddenly they stopped. There were no more letters."

"Your parents?"

"They're both dead. Mom died two years ago. She never was the same after Dad died." Then she added, firming herself and sitting up straighter in her chair, "Two years ago, the day before yesterday to be exact, my mother died. And Dad, five years back, he was thrown out of a wagon box when his team bolted, and was killed."

"Got any leads where your brothers might have gone? I mean why are you looking in Virginia City?"

"This is the last place they sent any news from. Or at least Dave did. Tom hadn't written for some months before that."

"Why did you decide now to come out and look for them?"

She avoided his gaze now, looking toward the window of the dining room. "It doesn't matter, does it?"

"Well, it might help if you know something," the Gunsmith said thoughtfully.

She was again looking down at her hands, and he saw the dimple in her cheek move. "You're an observant man, Mr. Adams."

"Call me Clint."

"Okay, Clint."

"Why?"

"Why did I decide to look for them just now? I'd been wanting to come, and kept putting it off. Then . . ." She paused, but only for a moment. "Then my engagement to be married broke off, and I decided to come out, I . . . I decided to do what I wanted to do." She looked up at him. "Does that answer it?"

He caught the sorrow in her voice.

"Do you still love him?"

She was shaking her head. "No. I never did. I realized that finally, and that's why I broke it off."

"I see."

"Do you?" She was looking at him intently. "Yes, I believe you do. Thank you." And then, lifting her cup of coffee, she drank a little. "Will you look for my brothers? You see, I wrote the authorities at Elk Lodge and then here too, but I only got the same answer from each place. They knew of nobody like that, or with the name Miller and the description I'd given."

"A lot of people take different names out in this country," Clint said, "and it doesn't have to mean anything bad."

"Will you help me?"

"Why me?"

"Because I trust you."

"Then you'd better tell me the whole thing," he said.

He watched the surprise sweep through her face. "Like I said, Mr. Adams—Clint—you are very observant."

"There was something back at the holdup, wasn't there."

She sighed. "I . . . I don't know. I thought one of the men was my brother Dave. I could almost have sworn it."

"But you couldn't be sure, of course, with the mask."

"It was in the way he moved. His manner . . . something. Oh, it frightened me, and I'm still frightened." Suddenly she put her hands over her eyes, fighting tears.

The Gunsmith resisted the all but irresistible urge to take her into his arms and comfort her.

"I'll help you," he said. "But please don't expect too much. It might be your brother, and it might not. I'll do what I can. Also, I have to tell you, I've a job of some sort or other in the offing and I don't know how much time I can give to this."

"It's all right. I understand. And I am prepared to pay you for your time and trouble."

"That's not necessary, ma'am. I'd be pleased to help such a lovely young lady," Clint responded.

Later, on his way back up to his room, he decided that what he liked so much about Miss Sally Miller, besides her undoubted physical attributes, was her quiet containment, the sense of a very youthful maturity.

SIX

It was cute. Delayed action. And had the girl known all along? Cute, he told himself again as he stood in his hotel room examining the damage. His left hand was again swollen, he had a cut along his chest, not very deep, and his head was hammering.

They'd been waiting in the room when he came back upstairs after seeing Sally Miller. Three of them. The room had been almost dark, the gray light helping to conceal them.

Funny, that funny feeling just before he'd opened the door—and then something hit him right in the jaw and they had him down on the floor. If he hadn't remembered the chamber pot under the crazy bed, he might have been finished right there. But in the nick of time he reached out, grabbed it by its handle, and smashed it over somebody's head. It gave him the moment he needed to get up onto his knees and strike out with his fists. Then he was on his feet. The next assailant he kicked right smack in the balls, downing him like a foundered horse, gagging, spewing, and clutching in agony. That left the third man, who had raced to the door to escape. He'd just gotten his hand on the jamb when the Gunsmith slammed the door. The man's scream cut through the Boston House like a razor.

Meanwhile doors were banging up and down the corridor, men were cursing, and there was a pounding of feet coming up the stairs. Clint yanked the man back into the room, slamming him to the floor. Quickly he locked the door, snapped on the light, drew his gun. His attackers were still on the floor. All the fight had been knocked out of them.

"Who sent you?" he demanded of the three fallen attackers. One man was spitting out blood and teeth, another was clutching his groin, while the third was trying to hold his smashed hand, but it was too painful to even touch.

"I said, who sent you sonsofbitches!" And the click of the hammer drawing back beneath his thumb was the only sound in the next split second.

"Dutch . . ." babbled the one with the smashed hand.

"Shut up, you stupid bastard!" snarled the man who had taken the chamber pot across his head.

This remark was followed by a great banging on the door.

"Who is it?" snapped the Gunsmith.

"Marshal Doanes! You open up!"

A short man who looked as though he was made out of wire stood framed in the doorway when Clint opened it.

"What the hell's going on in here?" The voice matched the body, twanging out the words.

"Just celebrating my birthday, Marshal. These are uninvited guests. Want to take 'em?"

"I am taking 'em down to the lockup—and you, too, mister."

"Why me? These men attacked me. This is my room."

Suddenly a voice spoke from behind the Virginia City marshal.

"I am looking for Clint Adams. Is this his room?"

A knobby man in a tight beard and mustache worked his way carefully around the marshal, nodding and offering a casual "Hello." And then to the Gunsmith, "Are you Clint Adams?"

"Who wants to know?"

"I'm Clem Hollinger from Wells, Fargo. Mr. Holbrook sent me to see if you'd arrived yet. The clerk downstairs—"

"Everybody in the whole town seems to be interested in whether I've arrived or not," Clint snapped. "Shit, I even had a welcoming committee out on the road."

"Such is fame," Hollinger said. "Marshal, this is Clint Adams."

"I figured that out by now, for Christ sake, Hollinger," snarled the marshal, whose tight eyes were pecking over the three woebegone men who were now up on their feet.

Hollinger ignored the sarcasm as he swept on. "And I'll take responsibility for him."

"You will when I release him, mister!" snapped Doanes. "I got some questions on this and on a holdup I just heard about."

Hollinger sighed. "Marshal, can't I vouch for Adams? He's come here on Wells, Fargo business. I promise to bring him down to your office after he sees Holbrook. Say in the morning.''

"Shit," said the marshal.

"I don't want to say any more in front of these men," Hollinger added.

"Make sure about it then. And you, Adams. I want to know about the stage holdup."

"I stopped by your office when we got in, Marshal. There wasn't anybody there so I figured on looking you up in the morning," Clint said easily.

"I will see you in the morning," Marshal Doanes said.

Hollinger was clearly a man with a sense of humor. "Welcome to Virginia City, Adams."

"Thanks," replied the Gunsmith, his tone wry. He had walked to the washstand, poured water, and was washing his face and hands. His ribs hurt and his head, but otherwise he felt good.

"What can you expect," Clem Hollinger said lightly, "when you're the famous Gunsmith?"

SEVEN

The Wells, Fargo office was not far from the Boston House, and they were there within minutes. A man with one eye was sitting at the desk, going through some papers, when the Gunsmith and Clem Hollinger walked in.

"Mr. Holbrook, Clint Adams," Hollinger said, and the Gunsmith noted the deference Hollinger offered his superior.

The one-eyed man stood up, offering a long thin hand over the disorder on his desk. "Well, you finally got here. Sit down. Clem, stay with us."

"Thought I'd come along, see what you had to offer," Clint said.

Holbrook grinned. "We were expecting you," he said. He was about forty-five, well built, with hands that seemed never to be still. Not that they were shaking, but rather always in kind of a searching motion. Now they tapped out a rhythm on the papers in front of him. Now they scratched at an armpit, rubbed the corner of his eye, traced a figure on top of a ledger as he talked. Warner Holbrook was considered one of

Wells, Fargo's top men. And he was. Clint Adams had heard of him.

"But you aren't the only one expecting me."

"There were some boys trying to rough him up in the Boston House," Hollinger explained. "I think they regret it," he added with a chuckle.

Holbrook nodded at that. "And a certain character living under the name of Big William, also, I imagine," he said drolly.

The Gunsmith had to grin at that himself, the way Holbrook said it, winking his good eye, tapping with his restless fingers and looking warmly at him from the other side of his desk.

"So what can I do for you?" Clint asked.

Holbrook sat back in his chair and folded his hands on his round chest. "What can you do for us? Heh, heh!" He cocked his eye at Hollinger. "What can he do for us!" Suddenly, swift as a cat, he sat forward, tapping into the pile of papers with his long middle finger. "You can do a lot or a little, Mr. Adams. You can help pull Wells, Fargo out of big trouble." He was still tapping his long, hard finger as papers began to skewer to the floor. He paid no notice. "I'm in charge of this division for the company, and we're being robbed blind. Blind! Someone's informing on our gold and silver shipments, and a thoroughly organized gang is by God running a business—a business! And at our expense! This keeps up, we're going to go broke! You follow me?"

"I follow you."

"We'll pay you, and we'll bonus any extras."

"I've sort of taken on a job already," Clint said easily. "Might be tight for time, Holbrook."

"You write your own ticket, Adams. I know your

reputation. I'll let you do it your way. Just get me who's at the back of all this and we'll bust 'em once and for all. Like I say, you name it and you've got it.'' He sat back suddenly, and in the next breath added, "I mean, uh, within reason."

The three of them chuckled at that. In the end Clint agreed to take on the job, figuring it might work in with his search for Sally Miller's brothers. He stood up, adjusting his Stetson hat so it slanted forward on his head.

"You know anybody named Miller? Tom or Dave Miller? They likely been around this country a good year or two."

The two men looked at each other, shaking their heads. "Of course, those could be summer names," Hollinger said.

"Sure could." He started toward the door. Then, with his hand on the doorknob, "Ever hear of a feller named Starch?"

Again the same response from Hollinger and Holbrook.

"Just keep it unofficial about me," Clint said. "I favor my privacy."

"We're agreed on it."

Warner Holbrook stood up and came around to the front of his loaded desk. He held out his hand. "I sure am glad to meet the Gunsmith after all these years. And I will know you only as Clint Adams. And don't worry about Marshal Doanes: I'll straighten things out with him."

Clint nodded. He closed the door firmly but quietly behind him.

EIGHT

It was becoming more and more annoying. Yet how could it be avoided? He hadn't wanted it—his reputation, his name: the Gunsmith. It was a newspaperman who pinned it on him, referring not to his vast knowledge of guns, but to his ability as a shooter. Clint Adams was not the sort of man to mull over the past or worry about the future, but he sincerely wished that the reputation building around his name would subside, dissolve, just go away. More and more he was aware of becoming the legend he sought so hard to avoid. And so, he'd become a target for any slaphappy kid who wanted to build a rep as the killer of the Gunsmith. And not just the kids. There were real pros about; professionals with amateur brains who would just love to best him in a "gunfight"; and whether the fight would be fair or not was not the question.

No matter; he had his hands full. The Wells, Fargo offer; the invitation to meet—sooner or later, and probably sooner—Hercules Rowayton; the girl and her missing brothers. And once again he found himself thinking of the man in the black suit with the black stovepipe hat and the penetrating black eyes

Trying to sort out his thoughts, he decided on a walk through town. The main street in particular was packed with people, horses, dogs, mules, noise, and dust; not to mention the heat, the stink of sweat, the jingling of harness bells, the wrenching squeal of wagon wheels on rock, the cracking of the mule drivers' thirty-foot blacksnake whips as they bullied their way through the town.

The Gunsmith walked past a tent that was almost swamped by a crowd of men listening to a mine representative recruiting labor. Another tent barker close by was trying to get workers for some of the wood ranches near Lake Tahoe. Restaurants and bars were begging passersby to become cooks, waiters, bartenders. A tailor's sign in the unglassed window of a log cabin asked for help.

Clint Adams paused in front of a frame building that carried a sign announcing it was a broker's office. A crowd of spectators pushed around a bulletin board reading the latest quotations on mine shares. The prices were sky high. It seemed everybody was speculating, no holds barred. As Warner Holbrook had said, the shipments would tempt heaven, Clint thought, let alone the other place. There were more road agents about than men digging gold. After all, why mine with a pick and shovel when you could get it with a couple of guns and a fast horse? But what really bothered the company was the fact that somebody had organized the gangs, or at least the bulk of the bandits. Someone was running a master plan and making a killing.

"They know our schedules more often than not—when we're making a big shipment, and almost its value. Someone's been working on the inside, and 've got the best horses, crack gunmen, and someone behind them with a careful brain.''

The Gunsmith had easily read the near desperation in Holbrook's words. Nor did the Wells, Fargo man appear to be the type who dramatized. Clint was convinced he wasn't exaggerating. And now, studying the crowd, reading the quotes on the bulletin board, feeling the tempo of the wild town, he knew that Warner Holbrook hadn't been laying it on. It was so. The whole Comstock was wide open, and somebody was truly making a killing.

Someone, too, was interested in another kind of killing, the Gunsmith thought, realizing he was being followed. As Clint turned he saw him moving back around the corner of a building. It was nobody he recognized; medium-sized, stocky, young.

He walked farther down the street, now and again looking back but seeing no further sign of anyone who might be following him.

Pausing outside the Wells, Fargo office, he overheard a driver talking to a man holding a corncob pipe, informing him that he'd just driven down to San Francisco with one full ton of bullion in his stage.

"Twenty bars of the stuff, by God! Most all silver, but it had enough gold in it to come to two thousand a bar!"

The Gunsmith knew that a large part of the public hadn't heard much about bullion shipments. Thus far the mills were making no effort to separate gold from silver, which was an intricate process. They were simply melting down the gold and silver in the ore together, pouring the resulting combination of metals into bars that weighed about a hundred pounds each. Each bar's value was then tested in Francisco, the determining factor being the of gold content. The more gold content, the higher the value.

"Weren't you afraid of road agents?" the Gunsmith asked, suddenly butting in. "Couldn't help but overhear you, mister. Sounds like a helluva lot of dollars there."

The driver grinned, revealing a wide gap where some teeth were missing. "Shit, no. They can't handle bullion 'thout wagons 'n' pack animals. They'd sure as hell be slowed down. Besides, the mining company's got its name cast right into the bar, and that's one brand, by God, you can't change!"

The Gunsmith spotted him again, this time dodging into a tent. He was certain it was the same man he'd seen before. Well, he decided, no point in playing games. Let's flush the bugger.

Turning in the direction of his rooming house, he felt relieved that he'd come to a decision, for he knew from long experience that a man could think himself silly. A little thinking was necessary, sure, but too much and you got holes in your head; that's to say, a man could lose his sharpness. The Gunsmith was a man for action—tempered, not muddied, by thought. He'd see who this bird was—from Hercules Rowayton? By golly, that man was beginning to crowd him. He could still feel some of the bruises he'd collected in his hotel room.

He stepped along faster now, only he wasn't heading for the Boston House any longer. He was heading for the Silver Dollar Bar and Gaming Establishment. The Silver Dollar, Ginger had told him, was where she plied her trade.

NINE

The Silver Dollar was a two-bit bar instead of a short-bit establishment, meaning that the drinks were twenty-five cents or two long bits, instead of one short bit, ten cents. This exclusive pricing eliminated the riffraff. Indeed, the place was as quiet and refined as any in San Francisco—which, to be sure, still gave it a good bit of leeway. The fifty-foot mirror and the mahogany bar had been shipped by clipper ship around the horn from New York, then freighted from San Francisco by mule team. The coal-oil lamps with their gleaming reflectors had also made the journey. The contrast of all this elegance against the rough log walls under a pine-board ceiling held up by unpeeled log pillars, would have been startling to anyone who took the time to notice. Few did.

Clint ordered the usual drink in that part of the country, a beverage known as tarantula juice. He looked around at the other men at the bar. About fifteen or so were lined up at the brass foot rail, and perhaps the same amount were seated in small groups at various tables. He picked them for mine superintendents, speculators, brokers, lawyers.

He saw him then in the big mirror at the same time that he spotted Ginger. In fact, she and the man following him exchanged glances. It was all the Gunsmith needed. Clearly the man was also working for Rowayton. Turning, Clint smiled at Ginger as she walked toward him.

She was wearing a green satin gown, and most of her breasts weren't in it. He felt his organ like a stick in his trousers. It was instantaneous. But he cautioned himself to control his passion; this was a moment for business, not pleasure.

"Feel like some company?" she said, glancing upstairs, where a girl and an obviously happy man were just passing along the balcony. "Any time. And . . . uh"—with the tip of her tongue pointing between her teeth—"there's no charge. I mean, just between you and me."

"Of course," the Gunsmith said, his erection tearing at his trousers. Out of the side of his eye he saw the man quickly look away; then he was following the girl's satin-covered buttocks up the stairs.

The room was a bed and a washstand. The moment they were inside she spun around and locked the door.

"Listen, I'm a damn fool for telling you this, but I can't help it. Rowayton is after you. He's got someone following you now."

"I figured that."

"Yes, but there's more. He's setting you up. The thing is, he's the kind who never takes no. You'd better go see him, listen to what he has to offer. That's all he wants—you to come to him. You get it?"

She was standing tensely before him, her breath coming quickly out of her parted lips.

"I was figuring to pay him a visit. But like I said, I've been pretty busy since getting into town," he said with a chuckle.

"Clint, that man who's following you—he isn't going to do anything. He'll just report to Rowayton on your moves. So there's nothing to worry about, really. Just be careful, okay? And get your ass over to see Rowayton."

"Okay, okay. Now, how about that offer of pleasure," he said seductively, as he began to remove her dress.

TEN

"Why didn't you kill him?" Hercules Rowayton stood in front of the dark man in dark clothes. The light coming through the office window was bleak. It was morning, and rough weather was expected.

"On account of the girl." Starch's tone was surly; it usually was. "And on account of you told me not to. Not yet."

Rowayton looked at the dark circles under the other man's eyes. "I am glad you used your head there. It would have been most unfortunate if the girl had been killed, and even worse if she'd witnessed something she shouldn't."

"I'll get him," Starch said, staring at the window.

"I know you will. But first you're going to just stay close. Let him wonder. You understand? We want to get him off balance."

"Huh?" A new expression came slowly to Starch's face, which his employer decided was one of interrogation.

"You want to know why." It was a statement, and it led to the next thing Rowayton wished to say. "I discovered that Wells, Fargo had invited Adams to investigate the rash of robberies around here. Knowing the Gunsmith's reputation, I decided to forestall such an investigation. And this is where you come in. But we have to play it careful. No one—I repeat, no one—is to know that you and I have any connection with each other.''

''Hah.'' Starch opened his big mouth to yawn, revealing brown stumps, a pale, coated tongue, and foul breath.

Hercules Rowayton winced. ''When you defeat Mr. Adams in the classic Western gun duel you will then be the Number One gunfighter of the Great American West! Think of that !''

''Huh . . .'' muttered the granite Starch. His face twisted, some kind of grimace appeared, and Hercules Rowayton realized that the man was smiling.

Starch was flexing his fingers, holding his hands in front of him, close to his chest. He was actually grinning now, his wide mouth sliced open across his big face like a cut in a melon. There was no humor in it, and Rowayton—though definitely a man of the world, and no softy—felt a moment of queasiness.

He controlled himself, and said, ''I don't want you doing anything to Adams until I give you the word. You understand?''

Starch emitted a sound from deep in his throat.

''Do you understand me!''

Starch nodded. His slanting forehead was damp with sweat as he left the room, the grin still cutting across his face.

Hercules Rowayton kept a small ranch in the Truckee Valley, a few miles east of Reno, along with three hundred fifty head of cattle and about two dozen cow ponies. Originally the herd and ponies had been brought up from Texas, but the owner, having arrived in mining country, swiftly caught gold fever and saw no sense at all in dealing with cows when he could make a fortune on the Comstock.

Hercules, to be sure, had his special reasons for buying the ranch. It was a perfect cover for the operation he had in mind, which was robbing stage-coaches and anyone or anything else that came to hand.

He had come originally from Chicago, but had adapted easily to the new country. The first winter, when he'd bought his ranch, was a hard one, with the price of hay going up to fifty cents a pound. The enterprising Hercules had made a small fortune selling beef to Reno and Virginia City. His ranch, protected in the valley, held grass all winter long, and when other ranchers discovered themselves unable to feed their horses, Rowayton was able to purchase cheaply the fastest mounts he could get. By the following spring his fellow successful citizens regarded him as the man who had kept them in meat, and saw him, too, as one of the most astute men in the ranching business.

All this was exactly what Hercules Rowayton wanted. His cover was seamless.

ELEVEN

After Starch had left him, Rowayton sat in his office in the big log ranch house, staring into his rolltop desk. The desk was crammed with papers. To be sure, he did most of his business in his head, and hardly had need for the desk. He wondered sometimes if that was why it was always in such disorder. It didn't matter. He was thinking of other, better things even before that thought had registered in his mind.

He was thinking of the money—the money rolling in, just for the taking. Easy as falling off a log. His plan had been so simple. He had his men all over the place. Clyde Skinnington, for instance, a talented bartender. Talented in the art of listening, of extracting information without the customer realizing what he was giving away. He'd sent for Clyde, who had been bartending in Reno. The bartender went to work immediately—due to an arrangement of Rowayton's—for a saloon keeper named Handsome Hinds, who was something of a figure in town. It took only a little while for Rowayton to win Hinds over to his enterprise.

Handsome Hinds wore a giant diamond stickpin in his silk four-in-hand, and the buttons of his black frock coat were huge gold nuggets. He was a big man with a big belly, and in the local political scene his word carried as much weight as his fist did with the local boozers.

Handsome favored girls in his saloon, and he also liked music—he kept two six-piece orchestras playing continuously, that is, taking turns. For the miners the accordion was the favorite instrument, and it was generally backed up by the banjo for dancing; the guitar, the fiddle, and now and again a drum and a cornet added to the festivities. The girls were eager for work, the miners thirsty and horny. With the music pounding out hour after hour, the Silver Dollar was the busiest spot in town, a place Rowayton knew would carry much gossip, where a quick bartender such as Clyde Skinnington could learn many fascinating bits and pieces; most of which Hercules Rowayton could work into a neat pattern that always meant money.

At the same time, when payment for drinks was made in gold dust a shrewd employee could scoop up a little extra for himself when weighing the dust on the scale, provided he let his little fingernail grow long enough. However, Clyde Skinnington added a wrinkle to the trick. He not only had a good speaking voice that attracted a customer's confidence, but he also sported a good head of hair. And he had the habit, when reckoning out the precise weight of the gold being paid, of running his fingers through his hair as an aid to concentration. "Got to be careful to make it the exact balance," he'd say. And the customers all chuckled at that, appreciating Clyde's honesty and concern, some laughing a little extra, too, as they saw how he tended to be nervous. All that fidgeting!

Later, when his time to take a break came, Clyde would address himself to a washbowl in his room and wash out his hair. The take in gold dust was usually a good one.

But he could also forward to Rowayton such information that included tips on mining stocks, habits of stagecoach drivers, bullion shipping schedules, payroll schedules, who was going down to California and who was coming back, movements of geologists and engineers that might indicate a new discovery. In short, nothing was too big or too small to be discussed and noted for future reference.

Yes, everything had been going well, Rowayton was thinking. And he wanted it to stay that way. But this action on the part of Wells, Fargo hiring the Gunsmith—he didn't like it. Not a bit. He'd heard plenty about the Gunsmith: He knew that he was one of that rare sort you couldn't bribe, couldn't browbeat and bully, and you damn near couldn't outsmart, or even kill. Well, he would see. Stash Hammond and his boys had buggered it, so had Cole Doonby and the Harrigan brothers, whom he was about to bail out of jail. The damn fools—not a one of them worth a can of cold piss.

At the same time he didn't want anything to happen to the Gunsmith that would attract attention to himself and his operation in Virginia City and its environs. And there was Starch. Well, maybe he would play his next card himself. He'd sent for Adams, but the man had made no move. Well, he would see.

TWELVE

The Gunsmith spotted the rider off to his right just a short distance from Rowayton's Four Aces ranch. And then another, sure enough, off to his left. Probably more men out of sight, he figured. He knew they wanted him to see them. Clearly this was part of Rowayton's strategy—figuring to throw a scare, to show muscle.

Clint Adams didn't give a damn. He had the scattergun lying across his saddle, just back of the pommel, which was why he'd asked for the big old stock saddle when he'd rented the tough little buckskin at the livery in town. Still, he wished he had Duke, his big black gelding; but he'd decided to leave him in Elk Lodge while he came over to Virginia City on the stage. He hadn't known how long he was going to stay, but he'd wanted to get there in a hurry because he was sure Big William would pursue him. He'd wanted to be ready, not caught on the trail and heavily outnumbered. The stage had seemed the best bet.

He had his slicker thrown over the scattergun, and was glad to feel the few drops of rain starting to patter down, for it gave plausibility for the slicker.

53

He smiled to himself, suddenly remembering an old-timer he'd known up along the Snake River. "The secret," Old Snake River Bill had told him— and everybody else he ever came in contact with— "the secret, let me tell you, is never to try to figger too much on what's ahead. You got to plan—that is for sure—but you cannot worry it. For if you're all the time thinking about how you're going to get out, you'll never by God move in; you'll be done for. Got what I mean? What I am meaning is a man has to figger he is done for already, and then he is shut of that concern. Like you're already dead, you got nothing to lose."

Now more men who had been in the barn and bunkhouse appeared on foot. With the horsemen there were about a dozen in all.

Clint Adams rode right up to the big log house and sat the buckskin quietly, letting his glance pass along the faces of the men in front of him, feeling the presence of those behind. Suddenly he swung easily around in his saddle, yet without being abrupt, so as not to startle anybody, and his eyes searched the group in the rear.

"Looking for somebody, mister?"

He swung back to face the speaker, moving the scattergun into a better position as he did so, but still keeping it under the slicker, out of sight.

It was a man wearing a big black Stetson hat, heavily creased in the middle.

The rain had stopped, and overhead the gray clouds were moving swiftly about, as though preparing to leave the sky. But nobody at the Four Aces noticed this. They all had their attention on Clint Adams and the man under the big black Stetson hat.

A charged moment held the group.

"I asked you a question, Gunsmith."

Clint let his eyes move through the group again. But it was too difficult to recognize any who might have been in the gang that held up the stage.

Another long moment passed, then the Gunsmith said, "I'm looking for Tom and David Miller." But he didn't look at the man under the big black Stetson when he said this; he kept his eyes on the group for any sign of reaction. He wasn't absolutely certain, but he thought he detected a tightening in a young man standing at the edge of the gathering.

"Nobody ever heard of them." The voice came from behind him, but he didn't turn.

The Gunsmith was looking right at the man who had questioned him; whose malevolent look seemed to take up the whole of his face under the wide brim.

"Then I've come to see Rowayton," Clint said.

The man said, "Mister Rowayton don't welcome strangers. You can talk to me."

The Gunsmith's hand was on the scattergun beneath the slicker, but he was leaning slightly forward in the saddle as though making himself comfortable. He spat over the buckskin's withers and squinted down at the other man.

"I said you can talk to me, Gunsmith. I'm the ramrod of this here outfit. The name is Wagner, Dutch Wagner."

The Gunsmith sniffed. "Like I told you, I came here to see Rowayton. I reckon you better let him know."

When he heard the movement behind him he said, "I have got this scattergun pointed right at your foreman's balls." Keeping his eyes fully on Dutch Wagner, he let the slicker fall away. He watched the color drop out of the foreman's face while his eyes went instantly to the men in back of the Gunsmith.

The Gunsmith's lips were hardly moving, but his words were as clear and clean as acid. "You boys back of me, you ride around in front here real easy, so's this thing doesn't go off." He waited hardly a beat and then he said, "I mean right now!"

When they were lined up in front of him he said, "You can all unbuckle." And when that was done he said, "Now you send someone to get Rowayton." He was looking right at Wagner.

The foreman's mouth was a slash of anger in his dark face. His eyes bore into the man on the buckskin horse. "You can't get away with this, goddamn you!"

"Mister, I am getting away with it. Now get Rowayton. I'm not going to say it again." The tip of those ugly looking barrels moved just slightly.

Still keeping his hard eyes on the Gunsmith, Wagner spoke.

"Harrigan, one of you two." And off to his side the Gunsmith saw the young man who had been at the edge of the group step away from the others. He'd been in the act of loading up on snuff. Now he spat copiously onto the hard ground as he stepped forward to go for Rowayton. Clint noticed now that the man standing near him was a look-alike, and from the way Dutch Wagner had spoken, Clint made the assumption they might be the Millers. He remembered one of the young men at the holdup taking snuff.

But before the messenger got halfway to the door

of the house, it opened and Hercules Rowayton appeared.

"Mr. Adams, I presume." And with his hand still holding some papers, he gave a nod.

"That's the size of it," Clint replied. "Call your boys off and we'll talk, unless you want them to hear what we have to say to each other."

"I'm not armed, Adams. You can see that I'm not armed."

"I, on the other hand, am well armed. And your men have been bothering me. That's going to stop right now."

"Of course." There was a tidy little smile in Rowayton's eyes and at the corners of his mouth.

"Tell them to get. They can leave their hardware where it is."

Hercules Rowayton gave a nod to his foreman, who was watching him closely.

As the men started to move, Clint Adams said, "Mr. Rowayton and I will be in the house talking. I'll have him covered the whole time. Remember that." He was speaking directly to Dutch Wagner, who was looking at the guns lying on the ground.

"Come inside, Adams," Rowayton said smoothly. "No sense being unfriendly. Nobody's going to harm you."

"I know that," Clint said as he swung down from his horse.

THIRTEEN

Just like other prominent Westerners Hercules Rowayton didn't carry a gun. Rowayton understood the simple fact that the gunmen of his time and place rarely shot important people, for the simple reason that such an act would not go unnoticed, and indeed would receive notoriety and swift retaliation, probably from the law. On the other hand he had no qualms about hiring others to engage in gun work. Thus he had hired an able crew of gun swifts to promote his growing enterprise on the Comstock—men such as Dutch Wagner, who were not only swift with a gun but also knew how to handle men. And, of course, there was Starch.

The hired gunman, dressed in black, sat motionless in Rowayton's office as the Gunsmith entered.

"I believe you two have met," Rowayton said. "Adams, this is Starch."

The Gunsmith merely nodded, and Starch uncoiled from his chair and without a word left the room. Clint sat down.

Unquestionably, Hercules Rowayton saw himself as an important man; and he was. But he also had no

illusions that the man sitting in the chair facing him
would find himself limited by such a view. A man
such as Adams certainly wouldn't be intimidated,
since he was no crazy gun hawk looking for a reputation. Rowayton had heard he'd been a lawman; and
surely he was no one to mess with.

It was why he was handling the situation with such
care, an approach he'd tried to get across to Starch
and Dutch Wagner. Those fools in the hotel room
and Stash Hammond and his gang had simply proven
the point. Adams was smart as a whip, fast as a striking snake, and certainly nobody's fool.

Rowayton had motioned to a chair with a rawhide
seat, while he'd taken the leather armchair in front of
his rolltop desk. Clint shifted his hat on his head but
did not remove it, and looked calmly at the man
seated at the big desk.

"Well, Adams, what can I do for you?"

"I've a couple of things."

"I'm listening." Rowayton pushed forward a silver box of cigars.

The Gunsmith ignored the gesture, and kept his attention on Hercules Rowayton.

"I'm looking for two men, young men. The name
is Miller. Tom and Dave Miller. Brothers."

"I don't believe I know them, at least not that
name." Rowayton had lighted a cigar and now released a cloud of soft blue smoke toward the ceiling.
He leaned back expansively into his chair.

"Could be they've got other names now. And
maybe they're not even together."

"Check with my foreman, Dutch Wagner. He
knows the men around this part of the country a
whole lot better than myself." Holding his cigar be-

tween his thumb and first two fingers he looked across at the Gunsmith. "I believe you said a couple of things."

"Somebody's been getting in my way. First on the stage, or maybe even before that back in Elk Lodge with a fellow named Big William, and then three characters tried to beat me up in my rooming house. Plus, somebody's been following me." He held his eyes level on his host, letting the pause stretch.

Finally Rowayton leaned forward and tapped the ash of his cigar into a shiny brass cuspidor at the foot of his desk. "And you are suggesting I know something about this?"

"You certainly knew something about the girl you sent me."

A grin swept through Rowayton's face. "Did Ginger beat you up?"

"It was part of the deal—the setup. The boys played a delay on it, waiting till I went out and then were waiting when I came back. Cute."

Rowayton's soft face was impassive, his eyes staring at Clint Adams like two bronze marbles. "Sorry, I cannot tell a lie. I had nothing to do with it."

"I know you did."

Rowayton shrugged.

"I know you did. And I know you don't carry a gun. That's also smart. But your men carry guns. What I'm saying is next time—if you're foolish enough to try a next time—I won't use my fists, or even my knife. You understand me?"

Hercules Rowayton leaned forward, his big body moving with ease to a position where his elbows were leaning on his knees. He was still holding his cigar as he said, "You're mistaken, Adams, but I won't argue the point.'' He took a drag on his cigar, released the smoke slowly as he leaned back again. ''Now then, I wanted to see you. Perhaps Ginger forgot to give you the message.''

''No, she gave it to me.''

''I see. Well, what I have in mind is to offer you a job. How about it? The pay will be good, and I need a good man to ramrod a big job I'm planning. How about it?''

''I'm busy.''

''It could maybe help you find those two men you're looking for. You'd be getting around the country.''

Clint stood up suddenly, but not abruptly. Rowayton noted with appreciation the ease with which the Gunsmith moved.

''I've got one more thing to say.'' The Gunsmith stood looking down at the seated man. ''You send any of your crazy hawks after me, I'll kill them. And at the same time, I'll be careful not to kill them too quickly, but to find out first where they came from, who sent them.''

Without a second look at Hercules Rowayton, he turned and walked out of the house. He was still carrying the scattergun, and nobody bothered him as he rode away from the Four Aces. He knew he was being watched though. Only he didn't know that two of the watchers were the Harrigan brothers, and a third was Starch.

When Tom got the dice, Dave covered a couple of his throws with big bets, losing one and then winning. Then, when Tom handed over the dice, his brother Dave came out with a nine.

Tom grinned, fingering the pile of twigs they were using as "money." The bunkhouse was empty, the men out working around the ranch. The boys, having worked the night shift, had this time to themselves.

"When it's nines and fives I like to bet on the make," Tom said.

"I'll make it for a hundred."

"Make it for five hundred," Tom said, and he picked up a pile of twigs.

His brother grinned as he called; and then he threw the dice with an easy swoop and snap of his fingers.

Tom, grinning, reached out and picked up the dice. As he tossed them over to Dave he said, "I'll bet a thousand you don't make it, buster."

David guffawed, counting out the "money." Then he threw, bumping the dice hard against the wall of the bunkhouse. They spun on the floor before settling. It was the six-ace, and Dave's cheeks colored red over his short beard. "Shit take it! I never spotted it."

"The switch!" His brother was roaring with uncontrollable laughter. "Dave, little brother—when you gonna learn? God Almighty! I switched in those flats just as easy as slippin' off that cute little Ginger's drawers!"

Dave reddened even more under his older brother's laughing words.

"Shit, I slipped in the tops, then the flats, like one, two, get it skidoo!" Suddenly he was serious. "What do I got here now?"

"Dammit, Tom, will you teach me?"

"That is just exactly and pree-cisely what I am trying to do right now, for Christ sake! Teach you! I bin tryin' to teach you things since you was knee high to a fuckin' piss ant!'' He looked at his younger brother in dismay. "Why in the hell are you so goddamn dumb is what I want to know!''

"Shit.'' Slowly Dave Miller picked up the dice and examined them. He just couldn't catch it. Tom had always been too quick for him; or really, he had been too slow. That was more like it.

He looked across at his older brother—the wide shoulders, sloping slightly, giving him the look of a man fast, real fast with a gun. Which he was. Just like with the dice and cards.

Tom Miller was still chuckling. Suddenly he stood still, crouching a little. Like a whisper he drew his six-gun, aimed it and pretended to fire.

"Fast, huh, kid!''

"Boy, I'll say!'' Dave's voice was filled with admiration, hero worship. He knew his brother drank it in. But it was sincere. He would have given anything, anything to be like Tom. It had always been that way.

"You sure you saw her? I mean real sure!'' Tom was saying.

"I was close enough to touch her; well, almost. And I wanted to. God, I hope she didn't spot me.''

"So do I. Shit! You see what happens when you go along on something without me. Hammond should've told me about the job too. The dumb shit!''

"What are we gonna do, Tom?''

"I dunno.''

"I had a feeling she suspected something. She was looking at me funny like.''

"But you had a bandanna.''

"Yeah, but she seemed to suspect something.''

''And that Gunsmith.'' Tom's voice had taken on a new tone as he said *Gunsmith*, as though it was special.

To him it was. The Gunsmith was tops. For now.

''What are you thinking, Tom?''

''Thinkin' about that feller.''

''The Gunsmith?''

''Yeah.''

''Tom, I know you're fast—''

''You bet your ass I'm fast!'' He turned, drawing like a striking snake.

''Swift as a fart in a windstorm, by golly,'' his brother said admiringly.

Tom Miller chuckled. ''So maybe . . . maybe one of these days I'll get a chance to prove it to you. Prove to my kid brother that his big brother Tom is the fastest gun in the whole of the goddamn country!''

''Tom.''

''Don't try to sweet-Jesus me, my boy.''

''I ain't. But I don't want—'' Dave stopped in midsentence. He knew how useless it was. It always had been, the time Tom had jumped into the river in midwinter on a dare; the time he'd outrun that crazy bull; the beating he gave Big Ike Dollin; and now the gun.

''Tom, what about Sal? Don't you want to see her?''

''I dunno.''

''Sally Miller is our sister.''

''The name is Harrigan. Remember that.''

''That's all right for fooling the law, but if Sal's out here looking for us, the chances are she could find us.''

"Why the hell don't she mind her own business!"

"Maybe she likes us, Tom." And Dave Miller—now Harrigan—felt the stinging in back of his eyes. But he didn't cry. No. Not in front of Tom.

"We'll see about it," Tom was saying. "We'll study it. Be good to see old Sal, but you remember we made an agreement, you and me."

"That we'd never let the Miller name get caught up in what we were doing."

"We'll study on it," Tom said again.

The door of the bunkhouse suddenly burst open and Dutch Wagner stepped in.

"You two, the boss wants to see you."

Tom looked at him carefully.

"That means right now!" Wagner snapped, and he left the door open behind him as he clomped out.

FOURTEEN

There was no question in Clint Adams's mind but that he wanted to go to bed with Sally Miller more than just about anything else he could think of. That didn't mean, of course, that he wasn't paying attention to his situation, or that he wasn't trying to fulfill his agreement with Wells, Fargo. In fact, he was leaning over backward to carry out the plan he'd set for himself with the freighting company.

The robberies were increasing each day, and it wasn't only the stagecoaches. Lone travelers were also easy prey for the highwaymen. Nobody seemed safe. Warner Holbrook kept emphasizing the difficulties of the situation to the Gunsmith whenever they met, which during the next several days was frequently.

"Clint, we've doubled the number of our guards, but hell, the road agents have tripled their forces. People around town don't seem to care too much, what's more."

"How come?"

"Well, they figure it's the big mine owners who get mostly hurt, and hell, all they've got to do to cover their losses is grind up a few more tons of rock. As for the people, the stage passengers, well, they're taking their chances. If they don't get robbed on a stage, they'll get it somewhere else. Actually, a lot of folks figure the free-spending road agents are a healthy thing. They keep money in local circulation instead of letting it escape out of the country.''

Clint Adams had to grin at that. ''But I see you've got notices up all over the place.''

''That's for sure—on bulletin boards, stage offices, and public places all through the country. Shit, they're so papered with descriptions of bad men and their stealing and killing, that passengers, and shippers, too, have got the notion that the most dangerous place in the world is aboard a Wells, Fargo stage. In fact, we're now starting to send notices only to police and sheriffs, instructing them not to post them where the public can see.''

''It does sound like they're organized, as you say. It's not random.''

''Somebody's tipping off the road agents, and it could be anyone. Except, of course, in the office here. I know all of my men, and I trust each one.''

The two men were speaking in absolute confidence, alone in Holbrook's office on a Sunday morning. The Wells, Fargo man had brewed coffee, and they'd been going over the situation for a good hour.

''What do you know about a man named Hercules Rowayton?'' Clint asked.

''Huh.'' Holbrook's heavy eyebrows shot up. ''Huh,'' he repeated. ''Rowayton's a big man on the Comstock.''

''I'm asking how honest he is.''

A big grin spread all over the Wells, Fargo man's

face. "Who knows? He's in mining just like about everyone else, and he doesn't use a pick and shovel. He owns a stamp mill, a silver mine, got a ranch down on the Truckee. The stamp mill's in Six Mile Canyon and it produces mucho bullion. My investigations figure about six to eight bars a month. He bought the mill cheap, I understand. When he started he was only bringing out a bar a month, but it's building."

"Anybody—yourself, or anyone you know—seen the place?"

Holbrook was shaking his head. "No. There's hardly a mine in the Comstock that doesn't have certain drifts the owners carefully guard," he explained. "And rightly so. Hell, if the ore bodies in those drifts proved of special value, the insiders—as you can figure—would want a chance to gobble as much available stock as possible before the secret leaked out and stocks went sky-high. So nobody really gets close to any of the mines." He paused, studying the back of his hand, summoning further thought.

Both men were silent for a moment.

When the Gunsmith got to his feet, Holbrook said, "You got a idea?"

"Might."

As he started toward the door of the Wells, Fargo office, Holbrook's words followed him. "You'll be studying it, I reckon. But don't do anything to—you know—alarm the law unduly."

The Gunsmith paused at the door and turned. He was grinning. "You know, you just gave me a thought."

"Good to hear it. What have you got?"

"Maybe that's just the way to go, Holbrook."

"Way to go?" The Wells, Fargo man was thoroughly puzzled.

"Nothing seems to have worked so far."

"So?"

"So, like you just said, maybe we've got to alarm the law . . . unduly."

FIFTEEN

"Mr. Adams . . ."

He hadn't seen her when he walked into the Boston House, but as he stood at the desk to see if there were any messages, she suddenly appeared at his side. Obviously she'd been waiting.

He turned and smiled down into her worried face. "Of all the people I'm glad to see, Miss Miller, you rank first."

But her smile was wan. "Could I talk to you? Would you have a moment or two?"

"Want to take a walk? Or better, how about another coffee? It was quiet last time in the dining room."

He was already leading the way, choosing a table, holding her chair for her. The room was nearly deserted, for it wasn't mealtime, though there was someone sitting in a corner looking through the local paper. Clint made a note of the man. Was there something familiar about him? But then he was turning his attention to the girl, Sally. He thought she looked better than ever, even though obviously not at all happy.

She was wearing a lavender blouse that fitted her loosely, yet it outlined the contours of her firm, springy breasts. He felt his passion rising even more as he looked at the corners of her eyes, her lips, the little brown curl that turned into her left ear.

"What's up?" he asked. "I'm afraid I haven't come up with anything on your brothers, though I have been making inquiries."

"Well, I have nothing either," she said, looking down. "I had hoped . . . I don't know . . ."

"Was there something at the holdup in particular that makes you think it might have been your brother?" Clint said.

"It was in the way he moved. I think I told you."

"Well, that would explain why he wouldn't be writing you. Don't you think so?"

"It would explain why they both disappeared. If they . . . if they took up a life of . . ." Suddenly she was holding her handkerchief over her eyes, her body shaking with sobs.

Trying to comfort her, the Gunsmith was aware of the man at the other end of the room, looking at them.

"Come on," he said. "It's not very private here."

She gave no objection as he stood up and led her out of the dining room, across the lobby and up the wide stairs to the floor above.

"I don't think I should come into your room, Mr. Adams."

"Call me Clint," he said, shutting the door and locking it. "I told you. Remember?"

Then suddenly she was in his arms, and his lips found hers. For an instant she gave herself to him, her lips, her mouth, her whole body pulsing against his.

"No . . ." She backed off. "I'm sorry. I don't want to lead you on. But I'm not ready . . . really not ready."

Clint thought he would explode, but he controlled himself, his penis throbbing like a great hammer in his trousers.

They sat together on the edge of the bed, their passion subsiding after a long moment.

"It's all right," he said. "I understand."

"I'm worried. I'm really worried."

"I'll help you," he promised.

They were silent for a few more moments, and then they went downstairs. Clint already had an idea for a course of action. She didn't want him to walk her home, so he left her at the front door of the Boston House, then on his way to the desk looked into the dining room. The man who had been there before was gone.

SIXTEEN

"There is no question that our enterprise is a hazardous one," Hercules Rowayton was saying as he stood before the full-length mirror in his bedroom at his Four Aces ranch. Hercules spent a good deal of his time talking to himself, going over his intricate plans, and discussing other things—not only in front of his mirror, but when no one was around he would engage in such conversations anywhere at all. It helped him think, and assuaged his occasionally bruised picture of himself.

Now he was waiting for Billie and Callie, the two girls sent him by Handsome Hinds and toward whom he had developed an agreeable passion. Of course, he knew this had to be temporary, for the true love of his life—Sandra Lee Dorrance was on a visit to San Francisco.

As he turned away from the mirror he was thinking that he was the only stagecoach entrepreneur who had put the dangerous enterprise on a solid footing. Other road agents had come and gone, either unable to stand the hectic pace or to get rid of the swag afterward. A number of the less intelligent had come a cropper simply because they couldn't stand prosperity and in moments of drunken carousel had bragged of their achievements. But he, Hercules—and what an appropriate name!—with his ranch, his silver mine, and stamp mill, had not only painted an honest face to explain his wealth, but with his front had been able to explain his rapid turnover of horses and to melt down stolen bars of silver, recast them in his own molds, and offer them as products of his own ore.

His horse business alone was worth quite a bit. With the constant turnover of mounts, he was pretty sure of his men not being traced, especially since they always took care to paint out any noticeable markings on the animals—such as white feet or blazed foreheads—with a paint that could easily be washed out later.

Yes, he told himself, addressing the mirror once again, he had done well, extremely well for a poor boy raised in the slums of Chicago. He had done damn well!

When the knock at his door came, a smile broke out on his handsome face and he checked himself once again in the mirror.

"I'll be right there," he called out.

Already he was feeling the strong movement in his crotch in anticipation of Billie and Callie as he came out of his bedroom, crossed the little passageway, and entered his living room and office.

But the lively movement in his trousers subsided in a flash as he saw that it was not the girls, but the two Harrigan boys. He'd forgotten all about them in anticipation of the two purveyors of pleasure. With anger and frustration running through him, not to mention impatience, he faced Tom and Dave and the business at hand.

"Sit down," he snapped, forcing himself to bring his attention back to business, for what he had to say to them was of extreme importance.

As they sat there listening to him, he brought everything he had to bear on this point. There was no question about it—the Gunsmith had to go. No one —nobody—said no to Hercules Rowayton and got away with it. He'd told his mirror that, and by God he was going to tell it to the Gunsmith, with his goddamn reputation. He was going to tell it to the world, and not only to Mr. Clint Adams.

By the end of his talk with the Harrigan boys Hercules was feeling much better. This time when he answered the knock at his door he was not disappointed.

"You're late," he said to the two young ladies. But there was not a trace of irritation in his voice.

"The horse threw a shoe and our driver had to work on it, or whatever," the one named Billie said.

"Better late than never," Callie, the blonde, said with a playful laugh as she came over and put her arms around Rowayton's waist.

"I think we could go into the other room."

Laughing, they followed him into the bedroom.

"You know, I can never decide which one of you to undress first."

"You've got two hands, haven't you?" said Billie, her dark eyes twinkling.

"But he means he's only got one of these," said Callie, reaching out and fondling the great bulge in their playmate's trousers.

"But he has something else," Billie said, leaning over and pressing her lips against Rowayton's quivering mouth.

He had already lifted her dress and pulled down her drawers; now, dropping to his knees, he pressed his face into her damp bush, while Callie pulled his bone-hard penis out of his trousers and slipped its entire length down her throat.

Rowayton thought he would go mad. After a moment he came up for air. They were all three naked now, and on the floor.

"Onto the bed," he gasped, and getting to his feet pushed the mirror stand over so that it was right alongside.

Then plunging again into Billie's thighs, his mouth found her soaking vagina and began to lick it, trying to see himself in the mirror as he did so, but unable. Even in the light of such a fabulous failure, his ecstasy was undiminished as he licked and sucked and finally came rushing into Callie's eager throat.

SEVENTEEN

"Tom, I want to tell her. I want to see Sal."

His brother was silent, kneeing the little roan horse as they made their way down the thin, hard trail from the Four Aces. Tom and the roan were leading. Dave was riding a sorrel with a wide white blaze on his forehead. They were heading for town.

"She's likely staying at the Boston House," Dave said.

"Maybe a rooming house. People been letting out rooms a lot lately—with all the money, all the gold about." Tom's face was without luster, and he spoke as though not hearing what he was saying.

"Then it won't be hard to find her."

"What you gonna tell her about us?" Tom asked. The trail had widened and now they were riding abreast.

"Worry about that at the time."

"You know Sal. She ain't gonna like hearing of what we do for a living."

"Why tell her then?" Dave asked innocently.

"She'll find out, sure as a chicken's got no teeth," Tom said with finality.

"But we ought to see her, Tom. I want to see her."

"Later," Tom said. "After this business; after we're shut of this business."

"You mean the Gunsmith?"

"What the hell else?" His brother's eyes flashed angrily at him, and the younger brother felt their impact.

"Tom, what's the matter? What you so sore about?"

His brother was silent for a moment, sitting hunched in the saddle, his shoulders bent in anger. Finally he straightened a little. "That sonofabitch."

"Who?" Dave was puzzled. "Who—sonofabitch?"

"Rowayton. What the hell's he talkin' about—watch this feller? What do we want to watch him for? By God, I've got half a notion to call the bastard."

"Tom!" Dave's voice was sharp, older with sudden authority now as he spoke to his brother. "You mustn't!"

"Bull*shit*!" Tom suddenly screamed out the word. "Who the hell they think they are! Rowayton, Adams, they think they're better 'n' all of us, that's what they think! Fuck 'em! I say fuck 'em!"

"We've got our orders from Rowayton, Tom: We'd better do what he says, otherwise we'll just fuck up his plan."

"Fuck him," said Tom.

"Fuck you, Tom!"

"Fuck you, Jack!"

"The name is Dave."

"Dave, go fuck yerself!"

"That's your best offer, is it?"

And now they were both laughing. It was a game they played, and it had broken the heavy spell.

"Race you to the creek down yonder," Tom said,

and kicked the roan into a hard gallop.

Dave, caught napping, as always with Tom, kicked his sorrel and the two boys raced across the hard flat ground toward the creek.

The Gunsmith had made his plans carefully. Working on the ancient premise that if Mohammed couldn't get the mountain to come to him, then he'd have to go to it, he had devised his scheme. Or, to put it in the words of his old pal Snake River Bill, "To catch a bear you got to be a bear." That is, you had to know the bear's habits and ways inside out.

Thus, the man who disliked being called the Gunsmith stood on a street corner close to the Wells, Fargo office. He'd already gone through the routine of inquiring about schedules to Reno, where the Virginia City line connected with the Overland Stage running between San Francisco and St. Joseph, Missouri. He discovered that there were so many demands for seats on the coaches, that even with three stages leaving each day he'd have to book passage a good two weeks in advance.

Clint mixed easily with the throng near the stage departure point. The Wells, Fargo depot was a collecting place for news, gossip, mine listings, and much more. Often, when pieced with other news and gossip, the bits of information made a useful tapestry.

Although the arrival and departure of stages was habitual, the event always drew a throng. Clint easily melted into the crowd, just another inconspicuous rubbernecker amongst the onlookers. He saw the driver coming up from the stables with the empty stage and six prancing fresh horses, ready to take off.

He watched, feeling the crowd's excitement as the

Wells, Fargo strongbox was lifted into the leather-enclosed boot just below the driver's seat. Then the mail sacks were stowed around the box in the boot, and finally the passengers' baggage was brought out and shoved into the rear box. The baggage that couldn't fit was lashed to the top of the coach, in back of the driver, a lean, whipcord old-timer who sat indolently in his seat, chewing tobacco and spitting: He was not a man for menial tasks, but a man with a place of importance. At length four men came out, staggering under the weight of a big iron safe. With much swearing, a great deal of perspiring, and advice from some of the onlookers which was ignored, they lifted the safe between the seats in the middle of the coach.

The coach was sagging deeply into its springs. The driver, chewing casually, was clearly unconcerned, while some of the passengers looked a little bit alarmed. A man wearing a visor over his worried brow, and with sleeve garters on the arms of his wrinkled white shirt, now helped three women to step up into the coach, then moved quickly out of the way as the men passengers took over the remaining space. Two men who were left over were told by the clerk to climb up to the baggage on top of the coach. Finally, an armed guard wearing a brace of six-guns and carrying a shotgun swung up with consummate ease to the place beside the driver.

It was the moment the spectators, and especially a number of boys, had been waiting for. The driver shook out his whip, allowing it to dangle clear of the coach, and then in one smooth and flowing movement snapped it between the ears of the lead team. The sound was like a pistol shot, and the six horses took off as one. The coach sank back the whole length of its cradle springs, then cut forward as though shot from a catapult. The passengers were instantly mashed together in one grunting, gasping heap at the rear end of the coach. The men on top grabbed whatever they could, even each other. The spectators cheered. It was a sight that happened three times a day, and many of the spectators had waited a long time to witness.

Slowly the crowd began to disperse, and Clint Adams let himself move along with them. He'd spotted the man who had been following him the other day, and he had a notion he was the man he'd seen in the Boston House when he'd talked to Sally Miller.

Had Rowayton hired the man? Or possibly Big William had sent him from Elk Lodge—he'd already received news of Big William's promise of revenge. Or it could be both. Why couldn't Big William be working with Hercules Rowayton? Clint wondered. After all, the bartender back at Elk Lodge had warned him that Big William had known who he was, that he was expecting him . . . as Rowayton had expected him.

Suddenly, out of the blue, he thought of Bill Hickok. His old friend. He was thinking of how Bill would have enjoyed this kind of action—the gold, the gunmen, the fighting, and the girls. With this in mind the Gunsmith turned toward the Silver Dollar Saloon. He wished Bill was with him. Bill, a man to ride the river with, a man for any season.

EIGHTEEN

From his vantage point on a knoll Clint could see only two timber wagons struggling along the road; both of them were moving at a snail's pace and were relatively harmless.

But there was the coach. He spotted it at the same time he heard the crack of the driver's whip cutting the air above the team's heads like a rifle shot. It was coming up a long grade toward him and the four men he'd seen behind the huge line of rocks on the far side of the road.

The four spurred their horses, obviously timing the arrival of the coach so that they would meet it head-on right at the summit of the long grade. All were massively armed with six-shooters and shotguns, and heavily belted with ammunition.

So swiftly did they burst over the crown of the hill right on to the struggling coach, that for a split moment the riders and coach horses became a great mass of plunging, rearing animals. The driver and the guard both threw up their hands so quickly that the guard's rifle went flying into the churning teams of horses.

The road agents had everything covered. But when
the guard's rifle landed on the ground, it went off,
sending a bullet along the leg of one of the riders,
who screamed out in pain and rage.

Meanwhile two of the riders had brought their
horses right across the coach team, which was out of
control. One man reached out and grabbed the reins
of the lead horses close to their bits, snatching the
team down to a trembling halt.

"Get the box!" a voice shouted.

It came out, landing heavily at the side of the road.
Then the leader of the gang guided his high-stepping
dun horse to the coach door and shoved his hat
through the window.

"I'm passing the hat," he called out to the passengers. "I want it well filled, my friends!"

Despite the overcrowded interior of the coach, the
men quickly got out their wallets and watches and the
women removed their jewelry. No one seemed to
doubt the seriousness of the situation or that the road
agents would not tolerate less than all the valuables.

The hat, loaded right to the brim, was passed back
out to the man on the horse, who now backed off,
hugging his booty.

"Get going!" he snapped. "And don't look
back!" He was glaring at the driver, who had picked
up his whip. Clearly it was no time for trying his whip
on the horseman.

In just a moment the coach was charging down the
road. The men on horseback swiftly dismounted and
two of them began going through the articles in the
hat while the leader shot the lock off the strongbox.

It had become clear to the Gunsmith as the holdup
proceeded that the whole affair had been prear-

ranged, that the bandits knew what they would find in the strongbox. He could see that in their lack of surprise and totally businesslike manner. Evidently they'd been tipped off, as Warner Holbrook had suspected with other robberies.

He studied them as they stood there with their masks down, taking their ease before riding off. Suddenly he wondered why they were taking it so calmly. The usual behavior following a holdup was to ride off quickly in case an alarm was given, or in the event of other travelers coming along the road. In fact the two timber wagons would be coming along directly now. It was surely no time for lying about. Yet the four seemed in no hurry to get going.

Seeing the leader looking toward a stand of pine trees for the second time, the Gunsmith realized why the men were taking their time.

Big William, heavily armed, stepped out of the trees and walked toward the four men. He was accompanied by two other men, also heavily armed.

"Anything?" Big William's voice carried in the clear air and Clint had no trouble hearing him.

"Nothin'," the leader said. "Must be a false alarm."

"Maybe. We'll see. Good to check anyway. Wells, Fargo's got to be getting tired of getting robbed."

"We didn't see a sign of anyone. It was all easy as apple pie."

Clint could hear the grin in the man's voice.

"Good enough then," Big William said. "I reckon we'll ride on back to Elk Lodge. Shit, I could use me a drink of something to wash down that trail dust. Following that stage was right dusty."

The other man said, "I got something here might

help." Walking over to his saddlehorse, he reached up to the roll behind the cantle of his saddle and pulled out a bottle. Uncorking it, he passed it to Big William.

Clint watched the smile on the big man's face appearing like a great cave opening in his beard. Each of his companions also took a swig, and then with a laugh turned back to where they'd hidden their horses in the pine trees.

"Can't be too careful, can you?" Big William said as he raised his fist in a good-bye salute before disappearing into the trees.

In a moment Clint heard the horses departing. He waited while the four road agents who had held up the stage checked their saddle rigging, mounted, and rode off.

Still he waited, feeling uneasy about something. He waited a long while, then carefully moved back down to where he'd hidden his saddle horse. Quickly he mounted and rode back to town. There was still something bothering him, something nagging in the back of his mind.

Not very long after the holdup the Gunsmith was seated in Warner Holbrook's office.

"Neat," the Wells, Fargo man was saying.

"And clever. Whoever's masterminding the operation thinks of everything."

"Then you're convinced the road agents have inside information."

"I am." Clint rubbed his thumb along the line of his jaw. "I am convinced. I was already, but it's good to see the details in action."

"So Big William and his men followed the stage

from Elk Lodge, just in case. It shows they're suspicious."

"They know I'm working with you, and they want to be sure they've got backup power."

"I've got a notion you're working out a plan, Clint. Last time you were here you hinted as much. You've got a hunch."

"What I've got right now is more than a hunch."

Holbrook looked surprised. When Clint didn't speak immediately, he grinned. "People say you're a lot like Wild Bill, and I say that too."

"You knew Hickok, did you?"

"I met him a couple of times. I was around where he was, back in Dakota."

Clint Adams looked at the Wells, Fargo agent with renewed interest.

Holbrook spat suddenly into the battered cuspidor near his desk. "You're like him. I don't mean just fast with a gun, but you've got other traits he had. One of them being you know how to keep quiet. I do believe those agents—whoever's running 'em—is beginning to get a little bit scared."

"You really figure that?"

"Big William doesn't get called out on a job unless there's a lot at stake. I figure he's one of the leaders."

"I see what you mean." Clint stood up and readjusted his hat, running the back of his hand across his forehead. "Hot, by golly."

"Where you off to?"

"To do some thinking." He paused, then said, "Take that action in my hotel room. Whoever handled that didn't send those boys in right away—I mean when the girl was there, or even right after.

They waited, waited till everything had cooled down and I came back later—delayed it, is what I'm saying."

"I'm following," Holbrook said, leaning forward in his chair, his forehead wrinkled as he listened.

"Same thing out there with the stage."

"I'm lost," Holbrook said.

"They were following me," Clint said simply. "Not close, or I would have spotted it. But some ways off."

"Jesus, how could you figure that?"

"It's the way whoever's running their operation works—with decoys and delays." He grinned suddenly. "But I've got a couple of decoys and delays myself."

NINETEEN

Folding the note and placing it carefully in her handbag, Sally Miller stood up. She walked to the dressing table, looked carefully in the mirror to see if she was presentable for the outside world, and then with her hand on the doorknob stopped, opened her bag, and took out the note. She read it again.

Dear Miss Miller:
 I understand that you are looking for your brothers, Tom and David. I may be able to help you.

Hercules L. Rowayton.

Without further ado she put the note back in her bag and walked down the stairs into the parlor of Mrs. Sandra Dorrance's rooming house on A Street.

She entered the room so quickly that she had the strange feeling that she'd interrupted something between her landlady and the gentleman in the black frock coat, who was holding her hand.

The couple broke away, a becoming flush filling

the cheeks of Mrs. Dorrance while the gentleman, with complete composure, bowed courteously.

"Miss Miller?"

"Yes . . . Mister . . ." She blushed; she'd forgotten his name.

But the man was equal to the occasion, and chuckling lightly, put her at ease. "I am Hercules Rowayton. As you see, Mrs. Dorrance and I are old friends. It was through Sandra, of course, that I heard of your quest."

Murmuring the appropriate words, Sandra Dorrance left the room to them, then Sally offered her visitor a seat.

She surveyed the man who sat in front of her—the high forehead, the wavy hair, the clean-shaven jowls. A man in his early forties. Yet Sally wasn't too sharp at noticing further details, her main interest—her only interest—being news of her brothers.

"You say you know my brothers, or might. . . ." She was almost stammering in her excitement.

Rowayton held up his hand. "No, my dear. I must ask you to be patient. I wrote you that I might be able to help you. Let me explain." He leaned slightly forward, his eyes admiring her looks openly.

But Sally was too excited to notice. "Please, if you have anything, any scrap of information . . . I've been so worried."

"I have nothing certain. But I happen to have connections in town and in the surrounding country. I'm in mining," he added parenthetically, "and I have means of inquiring that—well, I assume you've gone to the law and all that—but I have means that are perhaps more accessible than the authorities have; I mean, since I am connected with quite a number of enterprises—mining, ranching, cattle, horses, and so forth.''

''I can give you a complete description of them.''

''Do you have a picture?''

Her face fell. ''No. Everyone asks that, but I only have something from when they were small boys.''

''How old would they be now?''

''Tom would be twenty-four, and Dave is twenty-one.''

''Any other relatives?''

She shook her head. ''Our parents are dead.''

''And, er, have you discussed this situation with anybody else? I mean, other than the authorities. Any private person?''

''I did speak to a man I met on the stage, a Mr. Adams.''

''I see.'' Hercules Rowayton dropped his eyes to his carefully cut fingernails. Of course, she would tell Adams about this meeting. Unless . . .

''Miss Miller,'' he said, looking up. ''I think I might be able to make some inquiries for you. But . . . it will be a delicate matter.''

''How do you mean, sir?''

''When young people come out here to the West they sometimes want to start a whole new life. Oh, it doesn't mean they've done something they wish they hadn't, uh, back home. But a fresh start is appealing to certain adventurous types, especially amongst the young. Do you understand?''

''I believe so.'' At this point Sally Miller would have believed anything, if she could only locate her brothers.

''So I shall have to be discreet. Also, in making inquiries about someone, it's wise not to foster suspicion that something might be wrong. All the more reason for discretion.''

"Yes, of course.''

"And so, if you wish me to help you—to try to help you—then I must ask you to promise discretion.''

"Oh, of course. But do you really think you might be able to locate them? You see, I don't even know if they're together.''

"I must ask you not to mention our conversation to this Adams person. Not to mention my name. Will you agree?'' His smile was perfectly charming, innocent, kind.

Sally Miller could only agree. "Of course,'' she said simply.

Hercules Rowayton rose to his full height. He was a tall man, she noticed now for the first time.

"I shall take the liberty of calling upon you in a day or two. Who knows? Maybe even sooner.'' And he took her offered hand and bowed. "Now, if you will excuse me, I shall pay my respects to Mrs. Dorrance.''

Surprisingly, that lady arrived in the doorway as though on cue. "I just wondered if you would like some tea or coffee.''

"So kind of you,'' Rowayton said with a little sigh, "but business calls. I must run along.''

Bowing to the lady of the house, and with a special look in his eye that only she saw, he took his leave.

When he was gone Sandra said, "Do join me for a cup of tea, my dear. You know, I'm so happy to have been able to introduce you to Mr. Rowayton. I'm sure if anyone at all can help you find your brothers, it will be he.''

Then, to Sally Miller's astonishment, she said, "You look like you need some relaxation, my dear. How about a few hands at cards?" Seeing the surprise and even shock in her boarder's face, she burst into a tinkling laugh. "I do shock people, Miss Miller. But you know, I'm a widow, and I have learned to take care of myself in a man's world. Besides, I've always loved cards. My father taught me. He was a riverboat man. Colonel Llewellyn Beauregard Dorrance. He's the only man I ever met whom I respect."

She had risen, crossed to a small table, and opened a drawer. Returning with a deck of cards and a happy smile on her face, she said, "Jacks or better?"

"I thought the whole affair was handled beautifully," Sandra Dorrance was saying later that evening, as Hercules Rowayton slipped her shoulder straps down to reveal her firm, creamy breasts.

"See how you can handle this then," he said, and he took her hand and guided it to his erect organ.

The next moment they were on the floor and he was entering her easily.

"Oh my, oh my . . ." Her murmurs were like little birds in his ear, tickling, teasing, driving him to greater passion as he stroked her, going deeper and deeper. Drawing himself out to the tip, she clutched him, begging him not to leave, and he drove down again and up high, wiggling his hips as the end of his penis rubbed against her vaginal lips.

They were still partly clothed, not having taken the time to even aim for the bed but having at it on the buffalo rug, as they had a number of times since they'd first discovered their passion.

Suddenly he flipped her over onto her hands and knees and entered her from the rear while she squealed with utter delight. Reaching under her, he handled each breast, supporting himself on his knees as now they began to crawl around the bedroom floor, he driving her with his great cock spreading her wider and wider until at last he couldn't stand it any longer and ejaculated wildly all the way up inside her.

They lay front to back on their sides, spoon fashion, as his member softened, got smaller, and eventually withdrew.

Sandra turned to face him.

"I want more," she said.

"I'm afraid that's all there is, lady."

"Oh, Herk, I don't believe that." And reaching down between his legs she began to tease him.

"God," he gasped after a moment. "You're so right."

It seemed to Hercules Rowayton that his three-year-old affair with Sandra Lee Dorrance was all that a man could ask for. He knew that like himself, she was feeding him half-truths much of the time. Much of this was to be expected, for instance, lying about her age and the fact that she'd married her husband when she was seventeen, when in actual fact she'd been married twice before and had married Dorrance—who had left her—when she was twenty-nine, though she claimed publicly that he'd died. Her present age was thirty-three. All of which Rowayton knew, for he was a thorough man and had had her investigated by a detective he'd brought in from San Francisco.

He, on the other hand, had also lied; principally

about his desire for marriage. The fact was, he had a wife in San Francisco; that is to say, a legal wife, but one with whom he hadn't had relations in some time. Though he loved Sandra Dorrance passionately, he had no wish to marry her. Yet he felt if he told her so, she would break off with him. He knew his passion well enough to understand that it couldn't tolerate a withdrawal, though he had his other women.

For Hercules Rowayton passion was inextricably intertwined with self-esteem. To be rejected—especially sexually—was for him the mortal thrust. It was out of the question, and could not, would not be tolerated! Yet at the same time he realized that his lady love was becoming more importunate, more demanding, more questioning about the promise he had made her. And he was running out of excuses.

In the days that followed, the Gunsmith felt his hunch growing stronger. He no longer suspected he was being followed, he knew it. Twice he'd seen the man who had been watching him in the Boston House when he'd been talking to Sally Miller. And then he had felt it again on the trail, as he had the day he'd watched the holdup of the Wells, Fargo stage.

He knew what he needed more than anything else for the success of his plan was a horse. A good one. With his in mind he took the stage to Elk Lodge, picked up Duke, and rode him back to Virginia City.

He didn't hurry, checking every now and again on his back trail, knowing he could confront the two trackers but not doing so because he didn't want whoever was following to know he knew about them. There was plenty of time for a confrontation when he was ready—when he'd decided upon the most fruitful moment to throw down on the trackers.

They had followed him to Elk Lodge and now were following him back. But this time he was riding the big black, and felt glad about it. Duke wasn't just a horse, he was the Gunsmith's friend.

In Elk Lodge he'd stopped in at the Friendly Times Drinking and Gaming Establishment but hadn't run afoul of Big William, though his presence did raise the eyebrows of the skinny bartender who'd spoken to him the last time he'd been there.

"You lookin' for trouble, mister? You've got it 'less you haul ass, and I mean right now. But that's up to you, Gunsmith. I'm not the man to tell you what to do."

Clint had grinned at the man's fake deference. But he appreciated his chance to talk with him. It was clear the thin man had little use for his employer, but feared him.

"Big William wouldn't be over to Virginia City would he?" he asked.

"Couldn't say." The bartender wiped the mahogany top as he talked out of the side of his mouth. Clint had to practically lip read to catch what he was saying. "But if you're about, the word'll get to him. 'Course, he might be over there in Virginia looking for you. Exceptin', Big William wouldn't go up against you himself. He would have help. Plenty of help. You watch yerself, Gunsmith."

"I appreciate your concern." Clint was looking right into the other man's face.

The bartender dropped his eyes, then raised them again to look back at the Gunsmith. "There was a gal back in Leadville. Her name don't matter. You helped her." Dropping his eyes, he moved away, following his hand buried in the bar rag as it wiped down the full length of the mahogany bar.

He'd sensed the two men behind him as he rode out of town on Duke. For a moment he had the impulse to work around in back of them and cut their trail, but that would only have given him the satisfaction of clobbering them. What he wanted was a situation he'd get the most from: Like finding out who was behind it all; who was masterminding the big operation.

TWENTY

Diversion, the Gunsmith had long known, was one of the spices of life. Often when he had a problem to think through he would stop at a certain point, wipe his mind clean, and indulge himself in some quite different activity, unrelated to the business that had been troubling him. Often it was cards. In the present instance he found his diversion in full swing in the Silver Dollar Saloon. As it happened, his diversion was a most fortuitous one due to the fact that his path crossed with that of Sandra Lee Dorrance.

Sandra Lee, to the delight of her male companion, Hercules Rowayton, and the continuing surprise of many Virginia City residents, led a double life. Few who met her as the quiet and thoroughly respectable Mrs. Sandra Dorrance—who rented nice, clean rooms to respectable travelers—would have understood the other side of this charming lady; the side that became Sandra Lee Dorrance who not only loved to play poke, but was in fact one of the better, if not the best player on the Comstock.

Hercules Rowayton knew it and loved it. It was a monument to his self-esteem that such a lady and entrepreneur had chosen him for her sexual favors.

When the Gunsmith realized the situation of the lady and lady gambler, he was intrigued too. Clint Adams's introduction to her was all that he could have asked for.

In the Silver Dollar the lady had just joined the game. As the Gunsmith stood amongst the group of people watching from the bar, he heard one of the men announce, "Table stakes."

Clint watched the lady's profile as she picked up her purse, opened it, and withdrew a stack of hundred-dollar bills which she placed on the table in front of her. All the other players, who were men, had substantial piles of bills in front of them.

"I've heard of this lady," the man who'd called for table stakes said with a smile. "You'd better look out."

Clint could feel the excitement in the air as men crowded in to watch the game.

"She ain't feared of them fellers," somebody in the crowd said. "Are you Sandra Lee?"

But the lady in question didn't pay any attention to the remarks. Clint could see she was dead serious, cool as fresh water in the face of those tough customers. There were six men at the table—a couple of miners, three men who looked like they were in the way of business, and a man who appeared to be a drummer.

The betting was brisk, the stakes high, and it seemed Sandra Lee wasn't doing so well. The competition was knowledgeable, stiff, and showed no mercy.

One of the businessmen won a couple of thousand on a pair of jacks, the second jack hitting him on the last card, while he had an ace in the hole. The drummer won three thousand on three jacks against the three tens in Sandra Lee's hand. The betting, Clint could see, was crazy. Certain that the men were reacting to their female companion, he had no intention of joining the game. And now, suddenly, Hercules Rowayton appeared as one of the businessmen stood up to leave.

"May I?" He was smiling at Sandra Lee Dorrance, stroking himself with the knowledge that not so very long ago he'd had the dead-serious lady on the floor of her bedroom, sucking him like a madwoman.

Clint stood at the bar, sipping his drink, fascinated as he watched the game become crazier. The betting was wild. Rowayton at one point bet a thousand on an ace in the hole, hoping to catch another ace.

The deal went to Sandra Lee, and she won three thousand in one pot with a pair of aces, against kings in one of the miners' hand. The other miner had a pair of queens.

The next hand Rowayton had a king showing, one of the businessmen had a small card showing and no one else had any face cards on the table.

Rowayton bet two hundred on the king and was called around the table. The next round gave him an ace, and everybody except one miner and Sandra Lee dropped out. The miner had a pair of sixes in sight. Sandra Lee had a jack and a ten of spades.

The pair of sixes bet five hundred. Sandra Lee called. Rowayton, with a king and an ace showing, called and boosted it one thousand. Clint figured it was his way of learning if the miner had more than a pair of sixes. The miner thought it over for a minute or two, then turned his cards down.

The way Clint saw it, the miner must have figured Rowayton had him beaten, or if he didn't, he had a good chance to pair his king or ace.

Sandra Lee called. Clint figured she had to have a pair of jacks or a pair of tens and didn't want to chance a raise into a pair of kings or aces.

He realized that the room had grown quiet and the crowd around the poker table had increased.

Sandra Lee Dorrance held the deck of cards lightly in her soft but capable hands. She dealt quickly. The fourth card to fall to Rowayton was a trey. Sandra Lee drew the queen of spades, leaving her with a ten, jack, and queen of spades, a good start on a straight flush, though even just a flush would beat Rowayton, no matter what he drew. With a small card showing, he could do no better than three aces.

With a possible flush or straight flush staring Rowayton in the face from Sandra Lee's side of the table, the Gunsmith knew Rowayton would have to bet plenty to keep her out. And he did. Clint had known he would; it was the man's nature—he'd been studying him now for some time. Nothing like poker to show what a man was, he reflected. And this added knowledge was going to help him.

Rowayton counted out five thousand dollars, and was totally surprised when Sandra Lee called. Clint knew she was gambling on another spade hitting her. Or she was bluffing. But, he reasoned, why would anyone bluff unless there was a good chance to win?

Sandra Lee dealt the fifth card to Hercules Rowayton, and it was another ace. Clint figured he had another ace in the hole, and he did.

Excitement ran through the crowd now as the climax built.

Sandra Lee's pale white hands flashed under the overhead gaslight as she dealt herself the nine of spades. She now had a run in spades, and if there was a spade in the hole, she had Rowayton beaten.

Rowayton looked at her hand, and Clint could tell he wasn't going to bet.

"All right, Sandra Lee," he said. "If you've got 'em, bet 'em." At the same time he began counting his money as though he intended to call her, no matter what. If he had three aces, he'd have to call her, Clint reasoned.

The room seemed to hold its breath now as Sandra Lee bet twelve thousand. Rowayton took plenty of time out to study the situation. He had three aces against a possible flush or straight flush. A flush would be sufficient against three aces.

The Gunsmith knew it wasn't the money Rowayton cared about. It was his pride; his pride, which was becoming more and more clearly his Achilles' heel. He hated to lose to a woman who might be bluffing.

Finally, after a moment strung out tight as a piano wire in the crowd, Rowayton called. A gasp went up all round as Sandra Lee showed her hand. She not only had a flush, but it was as straight as a string. On the one hand she won twenty thousand.

A babble of talk broke loose in the crowd as the tension broke. Clint was watching Rowayton. His face was gray, his eyes pinpoints as he watched Sandra Lee calmly count her winnings, the total of which for the evening came to a good bit more than the twenty thousand she'd won on the final hand.

The Gunsmith kept his eyes on Rowayton, who was watching every move Sandre Lee was making.

He was sure there was something more to his look than losing at cards. He suspected there was a relationship of some kind. Rowayton's expression became a forced smile as she looked up at him. It told the Gunsmith that the pair were not strangers to each other.

He turned back to the bar for another drink, and when his eyes returned to the card table, Sandra Lee was standing, closing her handbag, and Rowayton had vanished.

"I'd like to buy you a drink," the Gunsmith said, swift to take advantage of the moment.

"I think . . ." She paused, looking carefully at him, the tip of her tongue just showing between her white teeth. "I think I might accept your offer."

Turning slightly, her eyes swept the room, as did the Gunsmith's. There was no sign of Rowayton.

"It looks like you've been deserted," he said with a smile.

"I see you're one of those who don't miss much," she replied, laughing.

"You live longer that way," the Gunsmith said simply, and accompanied her to a table at the far end of the room.

When they were seated and he'd brought them each a cobbler, she said, "He might come back. Of course, he's pretty angry."

The Gunsmith shrugged. "If he does, we can send him away, or we can buy him a drink."

"Or," she said, "we could send you away."

"You wouldn't do that, would you, lady?"

She smiled at him and said nothing.

Presently she said, "I think this time I'd better go, if you understand, Mr. Adams."

"I do understand. And you, uh, know my name."

"Yes. You fit the description. I have a, uh, acquaintance of yours staying at my rooming house."

"So that's who you are."

"That's who I am. I've heard a good bit about you."

"I'm better at telling it in person."

"How about showing?"

"That's my specialty."

Suddenly she was serious. "I'm sorry. I got carried away. I must go and find Hercules. But please—this bit of information; he and I are old, old friends—it's between us. Agreed? You'll keep it to yourself."

"Of course. Let me walk you to your house."

"Thank you. But I warn you, Hercules has me followed."

The Gunsmith was thinking: he has me followed too. For who else could it be? But he kept silent. When they said good night to each other he knew she wanted him as badly as he wanted her. At the same time he was glad they hadn't run into Rowayton, and very glad indeed that they hadn't met Sally Miller.

TWENTY-ONE

"You understand me! I want men on him every minute. I want to know everything he does, who he sees, where he goes. Everything!"

They stood before Rowayton's desk and nodded.

"You will report to Dutch here on whatever you might need—supplies, horses, whatever. But with information, you report to me directly. Got that?"

They nodded.

Rowayton looked at Dutch Wagner, who was more than a mere cattle foreman or ranch boss. Dutch "handled the men," and Rowayton didn't care what means he used as long as he came up with results.

Tom and Dave Harrigan—born Miller—stood waiting. Tom remained cool, aware of the need not to antagonize his employer, but with some of his contempt showing all the same. Dave, on the other hand, had difficulty. He would have admitted that he was frightened if the right kind of person had asked. Rowayton was a mean, tough, unforgiving sonofabitch; no question. And that sonofabitch sitting in the corner with the black stovepipe hat and frayed black suit was enough to frighten a corpse.

"I want you to stay close as his shadow, but I don't want either one of you getting caught."

"We get too close, he'll spot us," Tom said. "That feller is no dumbbell. He almost caught us one time before."

"You keep close," snapped Rowayton, "but not that close. Use your heads. I want him to worry, I want him to feel someone's after him; but I don't want him to *see* anybody! You got that! This time you be sharp. You've been missing things!"

"Got it," Dave said.

His brother gave a slight nod.

"If you need more help, more men, you tell Dutch. Dutch will speak to me about it. But you try on your own. You get too many people on a operation like this, they can get in each other's way."

"How often do you want them to report?" Dutch Wagner asked.

"Every day, every twenty-four hours. Now, you've got the other ones on the other person, right?"

"Right." Dutch Wagner nodded, thinking of the curve of Sandra Dorrance's buttocks as she walked. It was a pleasure watching her. It hadn't been such a pleasure, however, reporting to Rowayton that she'd spent time having a drink with Clint Adams. He'd thought Rowayton was going to blow up. Dutch told himself he'd have to watch how he reported such things, to be careful not to become the target of the boss's rage. The sonofabitch.

"You two can leave," Rowayton said. "You sure you understand your instructions?"

Tom nodded again, and his brother muttered,

"Yup, we do," and felt the anger rise in him at the way they were being treated. He could well understand Tom's attitude.

He said so when they were away from the office.

Tom replied, "I might just throw down on that Gunsmith feller. Get it over with."

"Tom, you promised!"

"Promised what? What the hell you talkin' about?"

"You promised me if that feeling got too strong for you, where you couldn't hold it anymore, that you'd tell me."

"Ach!" His brother spat angrily at a pile of horse manure as they walked toward their horses at the hitch rail.

"You tell me why that man has us in there for a lecture talk like that when we been following that Gunsmith feller all this time already! What the hell's the matter with him?"

"He's extra mad on account of that woman," Dave said. "I do believe that's what's the matter. Adams having a drink with her."

"Shit . . ."

"Tom . . ."

"What?"

They had mounted their horses and Tom had started to walk his animal away from the house.

"I want to go see Sal. She's worried. I want to tell her where we are."

"Not yet."

"But she's got to be worrying like hell, Tom!"

His brother swung around in his saddle, his face hard. "I told you, we'll see her when this business is finished."

"But why? You mean after you try to throw down on that Gunsmith feller."

"What the hell you mean, *try*!" his brother snapped, trying to keep his voice down, for they were still close to some of the ranch buildings. "There ain't gonna be no tryin', by God! There'll be doin'!"

In the silence that fell between them now he calmed down a little. Then he said, "See, if we look her up now, she'll get all wanting us to be around and all that, maybe even go somewheres with her. Only we got to keep our minds on business. Me especially. I got to stay hard, dammit!"

"Tom, you mustn't. You promised. Something happens to you, it'll break Sal's heart. Look, it's all right we worked with the boys on a couple of jobs. Shit, that's the way things are out here. Everybody's done a little owlhooting now and again, especially when he's young. Like us. But going up against—"

"Shut! Shut your fucking mouth! Goddamn you, shut up! Goddamn you! Goddamn you!"

And kicking his horse into a gallop, Tom broke away from his brother and raced down the trail toward the town.

Back in the Rowayton ranch house the atmosphere was not smooth. Indeed, the only immovable object in the office, apart from the furniture, was Starch. He continued to sit with his back flush against the log wall, his black eyes like coals gazing on the scene. The scene consisted of Hercules Rowayton, his foreman Dutch Wagner, and a huge man who had slipped in just after the departure of the Harrigan boys. Starch had seen Big William around the country, knew who he was, had him sized up. Big William also knew Starch. But neither spoke to the other; Starch sitting in the corner like a coffin, Big William standing planted in front of Rowayton like a giant tree.

"I'm telling you, Herk, that things are slowing down. It isn't just around Elk Lodge, but all through the country."

"I know, I know." Rowayton waved his hand, shook his head with weary impatience. "It's the goddamn railroad, for Christ sake. They're all starting to ship by rail, not so much by stage any more. Passengers too."

"Shit take it," muttered Dutch Wagner.

Starch, true to form, said nothing.

Rowayton had stepped to his desk and brought out a bottle and some glasses. All accepted. It was suddenly a gloomy moment.

"It had to happen," Rowayton said, breathing out his first gasp of whiskey. "God, that's what the doctor ordered!" He looked over at Starch, who had downed his drink at a gulp.

"I hear the first train's due in any day," Big William said.

Rowayton raised his glass. Then, seeing that some glasses were empty, he quickly passed the bottle. Again he lifted his glass. "We'll drink to the Virginia and Truckee Railroad!"

"You mean, drink to their falling over their ass. Shit, Herk, how we gonna break into those goddamn railroad cars?" Big William was red in the face beneath his beard.

Rowayton was smiling. "I've got that all figured out, my friend. Leave it to Hercules!"

"But those trains and that express car they're

loading with silver bullion rolls over those grades faster than any horse. How we gonna deal with that, boss?'' It was Dutch Wagner, bursting with what had been worrying all of them for some time, with the probable exception of Starch.

Even Rowayton had been concerned when he first learned of the line coming down from Reno to Carson City, then north again around the east side of Mt. Davidson to Virginia City—fifty-two miles of track costing three million dollars. Fabulous! But Rowayton hadn't worried for long. He was not one to be defeated by any damn railroad, no matter if William Sharon and his kind were backing it. The Central Pacific and the whole kit and kaboodle could go hang. He was simply going to expand his operation.

''I have a plan, and we shall see it unfold presently. Meanwhile, let's attend to business at hand.'' He was staring at Big William.

The big man looked slightly uncomfortable for the first time since he'd entered the room. ''The sonofabitch caught me when I wasn't looking.''

''I understand that Mr. Adams always catches people when they're not looking,'' Rowayton said, and there was a little gleam of pleasure in his thin eyes as he saw Big William wince.

''I'll even it with that sonofabitch,'' William said. ''See, he used his boot. He kicked me. Afraid to use his hands. He ain't a fighter, Herk.''

Rowayton grinned openly now. ''No, and he doesn't claim to be, as far as I've heard. But he is something you are not—he's a thinker. He knows how to use his head.''

''Do you think he'll fall for those two following

him?'' Dutch Wagner suddenly asked.

"He won't fall for it. But he'll wonder. I've had others following him, as you know. See, with a man like Adams you can't be orthodox, you've got to mix things up; surprise him, keep him off balance.''

"I see them two Harrigans riding out,'' Big William said, swiftly seeking a change of subject. "Can we trust them?''

Rowayton's smile was icy as he looked at the big man. "I would not have hired them if I thought otherwise.''

Big William realized he'd put his foot right in it once again.

Rowayton hadn't finished. His voice was as cool as his smile. "They will surely be trustworthy. You want to know why?'' He looked at his company, excepting for Starch, who was apparently not in the least interested. But Dutch and Big William were, or at least they were playing the role.

"A man's trustworthy only when he wants something from you. In some cases it might be your silence he wants. The older Harrigan—which doesn't happen to be either of their names—wants to gun down the Gunsmith and be Number One in the wild and wooly West of the Eastern magazines. I've promised him that opportunity.'' He was looking over at Starch. "Not on his terms, but on mine. Besides that, I'm remaining silent as to their true identity.'' He looked from Dutch to Big William and then at Starch. He was feeling mighty pleased with himself as he moved toward the door of his office. The meeting was over.

TWENTY-TWO

The Gunsmith, to be sure, was quite aware of being followed, and he even realized the extent of the tactic. For instance, he knew who had been following him; knew that the purpose was to rattle him, steal his attention from more important matters so that at the moment when the enemy wished to strike, he'd be set up. He had to admit that Hercules Rowayton's tactics were sensible, or at least as a plan. In actual practice they weren't going to work.

Meanwhile, the Gunsmith had a counter plan he felt would be much more useful to his purpose than Rowayton's would be to him. Moreover, it was a plan that surely would reap fun for its author. And to add spice, the plan was a dangerous one. Jealousy was a fiery thing to handle, but it could flush the enemy. It might bring Rowayton out into the open. For by now Clint Adams was reasonably sure that it had to be Hercules Rowayton who was running the road agents, Rowayton who'd tried so hard to shake him with the attack on the stagecoach, been responsible for the attack in his hotel room, the men following him, and even back to Big William, if the bartender in Elk Lodge was telling it straight. He wondered now if Sandra Lee Dorrance was part of Rowayton's game plan. He thought not, and he was taking a long chance on that for his own plan.

"You know that William Sharon's pushing the Central Pacific all the way to Reno with a branch line connecting the mining towns to the main line," Holbrook was saying.

"About everybody in the country knows that by now, Mr. Holbrook, sir," said the Gunsmith with a droll expression on his face that made the Wells, Fargo man laugh and move his hands even more quickly across his desk papers.

"All right. It's old news. But what I'm getting at—"

"Is how that's going to affect the stagecoach business as far as the road agents are concerned," Clint said, cutting in. "It'll finish their business, except for dribs and drabs, though they can still do some damage."

"Thing is, will they try to switch over to robbing express cars instead of stagecoaches?"

"Likely they'll do both."

"The trains are much harder."

"But it's been done," pointed out the Gunsmith. "Right around the war the Reno brothers pulled a job near Seymour, Indiana—the Ohio & Mississippi Railroad. They boarded the train, walked into the unlocked express car, held up the guard, pulled the emergency cord to stop the train, then made off with the loot. They pulled a few jobs like that until they got caught and hanged by the vigilantes." He paused. "Thing is, others as well as the Renos always centered their attacks on express cars known to be weakly guarded, and usually on small local lines seldom carrying much of value."

"We're planning on running a treasure train," Holbrook said. "We'll have the express car like a fort."

"You think that'll stop them?"

Holbrook nodded swiftly. "The Central Pacific will be operating over a single-track line with a heavy freight and passenger schedule in both directions. It will be impossible for anyone to enter the locked and barred express car while it's moving, and any barricade they might put across the track would be a signal for the whole train crew to go for their guns. The road agents will have a bullet-proof locomotive and express car to go up against. It won't be easy."

"No, it won't be easy," the Gunsmith said, and stood up, still facing Holbrook, who remained seated behind his desk.

"You think they'd try it?"

"I know they will."

"They're crazy."

"It can be done," the Gunsmith said.

Holbrook had been leaning back in his chair, tilting on the rear legs. Now he dropped forward with a slight crash, and leaning on his desk with his forearms flat, stared up at the Gunsmith with his one good eye.

"Tell me how."

"Next time," Clint said with a grin, and walked to the door. "I've got a couple of details to work out . . . and besides, right now I've got somebody I want to see."

"I am telling you once and for all, Sandra, that I do not wish you ever to speak to that man again!"

Hercules Rowayton resembled his namesake as he stood in the center of the Dorrance living room. It

was evening, the gas was lit, there was the faint odor
of a good meal cooking in the nearby kitchen.
Rowayton was immaculate as he stood in barely controlled fury, confronting the love of his life with his
jealousy.

"I don't think I wish you to speak to me in that
tone of voice, Hercules," Sandra Lee said. "You
hurt. You offend me." With the end of her tiny
handkerchief she dabbed at the corner of her eye.

Rowayton was not moved by this display of emotion.

"The man's a scoundrel. A gunfighter. A woman-
izer! He chases every skirt in town! I'm serious,
Sandra. I want you to pay attention to me!"

Sandra Lee dropped the hand that had been
holding her handkerchief. She stood firmly in front
of Rowayton, her arms down at her sides. "I will not
be spoken to this way! You have no rights to me."

"No rights, indeed! Why, what have we been to
each other, for God sake? We have rights. I expect
you to behave in a proper fashion and understand my
feelings."

"Understand your feelings! Hah! And what about
my feelings?"

"I am talking now—no, don't interrupt!—about
the way you slickered that game."

"That game? What game?"

"You were dealing seconds. I could have called
you. Are you lucky I didn't!"

"You mean the poker? In the Silver Dollar? Sir,
are *you* lucky you didn't. I was dealing straight off
the top."

"Like hell you were. Who taught you the Comstock Shuffle?"

"Not you. My father taught me. But I wasn't dealing that. And you know it."

"I say you were. You slickered that game clean as a whistle. Actually, I have to admire you. A bit." He'd stuck his hands deep into his trouser pockets, and with his lips puffed out in a soft whistle was striding about the room. "By the Almighty, if you weren't slickering that game, I'm a two-headed monkey."

"Herk, listen—I wasn't cheating. You know I never cheat. Only a fool will try that."

"Lady, you were dealing the Shuffle. I caught it right away, but I didn't want to tell on you. I saw you pull those false shuffles with that new deck. I saw you dealing everyone from the top."

"That's right. I did."

"And yourself the bottom card. Each time— everyone from the top except you. For four rounds, right? Then I saw it so clearly—"

"You imagined it!"

"Then on the fifth round you started second dealing around the table, again dealing yourself from the bottom. Listen, sweetheart, I was watching every move. I know you. I know you inside out."

"Then, you smart sonofabitch, tell me why I didn't win that hand?"

A grin took over Rowayton's whole face. "So you admit you were dealing the Shuffle?"

"I admit nothing. I know the hand you're describing, and I lost a pot on it. So your story is nonsense!"

"It's not nonsense. That's how you set me up. You knew I'd spot it, didn't you?" He watched the color come into her cheeks. "You knew, and you wanted me to spot it, so that the next deal you could really pull it off."

"That's a lie."

"And if anybody—like me, maybe—had said anything or even looked funny, had anybody even looked suspicious, you would have lost the pot, as you did. So there would be no need to call you on anything. Then the next deal everybody is at ease—if they'd suspected anything before. You set me up, sweetheart. It was me you were clobbering. Well, you're by God not getting away with it. I want my money."

"I'm not giving you a penny."

"There is also a certain payment for my feelings."

"Your what? Your feelings? And what about our agreement?"

"What agreement are you talking about?" he demanded, his voice starting to go hoarse.

"Our agreement that we were to be married. Have you so quickly and so easily forgotten?" Her words had suddenly turned to vinegar.

She'd stopped him as though he'd been shot.

"Why do you have to bring that up now?" he demanded, rallying.

"Why not? You asked me to marry you."

"It was you asked me to marry you, my dear."

The color had whipped into her face as he came back at her. But already the wily Hercules had seen the need to shift his ground. He stepped forward and reached out with a mollifying hand to touch the sash at her waist—a gentle hand, like a small child. His face was crestfallen.

"Sandra," he whispered. "Sandy . . ." It was his pet name for her.

"You bastard."

But he saw that he'd won. He had no problem pressing his advantage. His hands easily undressed her, and now she began to play with him, unbuttoning his shirt, reaching down to remove his shoes, her arm brushing his pouncing erection.

"Herk . . ." she murmured as he bore her to her room. "We must be sure the door is locked. Sally will be back. . . ."

He slammed her bedroom door in eagerness, almost dropping the key out of the lock, and with his erection between her legs rushed her to the big white counterpane on the double bed.

In the room at the other end of the short hallway Sally Miller wondered what the noise was all about. She'd only heard a few isolated words, followed by a kind of scuffling and for an instant she thought she should investigate. But when she'd opened her door she heard a different tone to the conversation. Then she heard the door slam.

She lay on her bed with her ear in her pillow, thinking of her brothers, wondering if it had really been Dave at the stage holdup, and praying to herself—as she had ever since that moment—that it hadn't been him.

The Miller-Harrigan brothers were keeping an eye on the Gunsmith all right. And they were reporting to Dutch Wagner. Clearly, Adams was dealing in something heavy with Wells, Fargo; for they had noted he spent a good deal of his time at the company's office.

Clint, knowing he was still being followed, wondered why. Were they setting him up for a bushwhacking? Or did someone—likely Rowayton—simply want to know his business? Well, he would know about his walking Sandra Lee Dorrance home. And so Rowayton would likely have a double need for keeping on his trail—the Wells, Fargo business plus the girl. Clint assumed Rowayton was the jealous type, because anybody with that big an opinion of himself had to be. The Gunsmith had decided to play it for all it was worth, and enjoy himself in the bargain. Right now he had his plan of action going. The first thing to do was get out to Six Mile Canyon to take a look at Rowayton's mine and stamp mill.

It was a clear night as he rode out on Duke. He planned to reach Six Mile Canyon before dawn, make a dry camp, and scout the lay of the land in daylight. He knew the place would be very well guarded. But he had to see just how, and how many men were about, plus anything else that would help him fashion his plan.

He knew right away that the two men were again on his trail and would stay right with him as long as he didn't make any moves to cut away from them. They'd followed him for a good while now, and he knew they would be getting bored. It was why he hadn't bothered them. Let them follow, he'd decided, until they got lazy about it. Then he would make his move.

It was time to shake them. The moon was up as he rode down along the creek bank, protected by the trees. He smiled to himself, remembering the expression on Holbrook's face when he'd told him his plan.

"I need your man Clem Hollinger," he'd said. "For a job."

"A job? Sure, you can have Clem. What's the job?" There was the trace of a grin coming into Holbrook's face as he felt something extra in Clint's request.

"I want him to play a role. I want him to be . . . well, you might say, a dummy. I want him to pretend he's somebody."

"Yeah? Who?"

"Me."

The grin had come out in full force then. "It's okay with me, if he's willing to take the risk. You know, there are people around here who want to shoot you."

"I would never have guessed it," the Gunsmith replied, and they'd both had a good laugh.

Clem Hollinger, the short, knobby man with extra-large elbows, was happy to oblige. "Things get dull around this place, Adams," he said in his droll way. "I feel glad for a little excitement for a change."

The three of them had chortled at that wry humor.

Now, coming to the ford across the creek, he saw that Hollinger was already there. Quickly he kicked his horse into the trees, and in a few moments Clem Hollinger, dressed in clothes that resembled Clint's and riding a big black horse similar to Duke, rode out and followed the trail along the creek. The Gunsmith waited in the trees.

It wasn't a very long wait. The two riders came loosely down the trail. They were talking in a desultory way and he was able to catch a few words, enough to know their names were Tom and Dave. The coincidence struck him that they might be Sally Miller's brothers.

The next few words he heard convinced him that they were.

"Tom, you remember your promise now."

"Shut up, will you. I'm sick of listening to your goddamn baby talk!"

"You know if you get to tangle assholes with that feller they call the Gunsmith, you're in trouble."

"Shut your mouth!"

"And you know how Sal will take that. Tom, I've had about enough of this."

"You sneaky little bastard. You agreed like I did to take on this job."

"Yeah, but—"

"Dave, if you go tell Sal, I'll never speak to you again."

The Gunsmith let them get well ahead of him, then nudged Duke out onto the trail and began following. Now the moon was down and the sky was filled with stars. It was very bright. It was easy to follow their trail. For the present Clem Hollinger, who was in the lead, wasn't going anywhere near Six Mile Canyon.

The Gunsmith hadn't told Clem how far to go, but instructed him to wait for his signal; he had to see just how he would play it with the trackers. Now, realizing who they were, he had to change his plan. It certainly wouldn't do to shoot them, but at the same time he wasn't going to confront them without thinking his plan through. What was best for him and his plan, and what was best for Sally Miller? These questions were going through his head as he and Duke followed the Harrigan-Miller brothers, who were following the man they thought was the Gunsmith.

TWENTY-THREE

Sally Miller, meanwhile, had confided to an understanding, kind, Hercules Rowayton her suspicion that her brother David had been one of the bandits who'd held up the Virginia City stage. She'd gone to see Clint Adams but the clerk at the Boston House told her Adams had gone out the day before and hadn't returned. In dismay, tired of living with her worry, she'd turned to Rowayton when he called on her one afternoon. It happened to be an afternoon when her landlady was away. Rowayton had listened to her, then suggested they take a walk.

They'd strolled along the outskirts of town—he was an interesting conversationalist, she decided—and at length ended up back at the Dorrance residence. Rowayton invited himself in, and Sally, happy to have someone to talk with, suggested a cup of tea.

"That would be delightful," he said.

When they were seated in the parlor he said, "Well, I feel that you should take heart. As I say, I've made inquiries—rather extensively, let me add—and I feel reasonably sure that the boys will turn up. I have, just as I've told you, followed some suggestions, and I'll be in contact with you shortly."

They sipped their tea and Rowayton continued his conversation about his two trips to Europe—to London and Paris, and to Rome. Sally began to feel better. With both Rowayton and Clint Adams helping her, she thought, her chances of locating her brothers were better. Both of them knew about the moment during the holdup when she'd thought Dave might have been one of the bandits. The more she reflected on that strange moment, the more certain she became that it was so. It had to be him. But a road agent!

"He was, of course, only helping," Rowayton said, "if indeed it was him at all. I wouldn't worry. Out here young men turn to all kinds of adventures, sometimes for a lark. They grow out of it. Keep your mind at ease."

He moved his chair closer and was leaning toward her in a way she didn't quite like. But she was too much of a lady to jump to an assumption. Discreetly she moved farther away on the short settee.

Rowayton, a cool hand at business, threw caution to the winds in the presence of potential romance. He swept onto the settee beside her.

"Mr. Rowayton, I . . . uh . . ."

At that moment they both heard the front door open and Sandra's voice calling. "Anybody home? Hello . . ."

Rowayton made it back to his chair in the nick of time. His face was flushed, the crotch of his trousers extended, and his hands shaking. He made an admirable effort to cover, but Sandra was no fool. But she knew her man, and so she didn't blame Sally.

Later she had it out with him. And then they made up—in the usual manner.

* * *

As Hercules Rowayton's passion was being assuaged, the Gunsmith poked the barrel of his Colt against Dave Harrigan-Miller.

"Either of you make a sound or a move, I'll blow his spine into paper."

He'd slipped up on them in the dawn, while they were checking the rigging on their horses, getting ready to ride on after their quarry.

"What the hell?" said the startled Tom, facing Clint, and his brother, his hands far from his sides.

"Turn around and stand next to him." The Gunsmith pushed his gun hard against Dave, who almost fell as he took a step forward.

"How the hell did you get back here?" Tom demanded angrily.

"I've been behind you this good while," the Gunsmith said, and watched the surprise hit them.

"Smart bastard, ain't you," said Tom.

"Tom, take it slow." Dave had recovered himself and now appeared the calmer of the two.

"Go fuck yourself," his brother told him. "Come on, Gunsmith. Come on, I'm calling you. Let him go. You and me'll settle this."

"Don't be a fool, Miller."

Clint had pushed Dave Miller away from him and now stood facing both boys. He'd taken the precaution of removing Dave's gun, but Tom was still holstered. He wouldn't draw against the Gunsmith as long as Clint had his own gun in his hand.

He saw their surprise as he said the name Miller, but there was no denial forthcoming.

"You know your sister's looking all over the country for you, you dumb shits. What the hell do you think you're doing, playing road agent or something?"

"Go to hell, Gunsmith."

"When are you boys going to grow up?"

"Tom," Dave cut in. "Tom, drop your gun."

"Like hell I will."

"You want me to shoot you right now?" Clint asked.

"I want you to holster that thing and draw on me. We'll damn well see how fast you are!"

"Don't be a damn fool, Miller. Think of your sister. Listen to your brother here."

"You hear me, Gunsmith? I'm telling you to draw. I'm calling you. You backwatering?"

Clint could feel something knot inside him, something bad at the sight of Tom Miller spreading himself. The poor damn fool.

"You're a fool, Tom. Think of Sally."

"Think of Sal, Tom," said Dave. "For God sakes think of her, will you. She doesn't want to take a corpse back home with her!"

"Oh, you too, huh? I might've known you'd crawfish out. You always were a crybaby, Dave."

"You're the crybaby, Tom," the Gunsmith said. "You want me to die in order to prove to yourself you're a man. But nothing's going to prove that."

"Gunsmith, I said draw. You know somethin'? Maybe I could beat you with the gun in your hand."

"Tom, all I can say is you're lucky you picked me."

"What do you mean, lucky? I'm going to kill you."

"No you're not. You're going to see how lucky you are." And in that second the Gunsmith dropped his six-gun into its holster, and before the young man in front of him could even clear leather, the shot rang out and Tom Miller's gun went flying out of his hand.

The two boys stood frozen as the Gunsmith said, "See what I mean by lucky? Somebody else would have killed you."

"A lucky shot," Tom said. "It was a lucky shot." But he was clearly shaken by the Gunsmith's incredible shooting.

"Tom, for God's sakes!" Dave's eyes were starting out of his head at his brother's words.

The Gunsmith didn't say anything for a long moment. "Can anything convince you, you stupid asshole?"

He holstered his gun, but in the next instant drew it again and shot Tom Miller's handgun, lying on the ground several yards away where it had fallen from the Gunsmith's first bullet. It jumped now as he hit it, and again he shot, emptying his gun, each time driving Tom's pistol farther away.

"Holy shit!" said Dave Miller, his jaw hanging wide now as he simply stared at the Gunsmith.

Tom Miller stood crouching. "Your gun's empty now, mister." His hand swept to the shoulder holster beneath his jacket.

The Gunsmith moved so quickly that Dave later couldn't tell what happened. The next thing he knew, the Gunsmith had a second gun in his fist and his brother Tom's hand was frozen in midair, not even touching his jacket.

"This belly gun isn't empty, sonny," he said, and walked forward, slipping the gun back under his shirt.

He went up to Tom Miller, whose face was the color of chalk, and without a word reached out and slapped the boy in the face—once, twice. He slapped him hard enough so the boy had to take a step backward.

"That's two times you're lucky, you fool. Don't try a third time."

With the supreme confidence that had earned him his reputation, the Gunsmith turned his back on the youngster, walked to his horse, stepped into the stirrup and mounted.

He sat his horse, looking down at them. "Who are you working for? Rowayton?"

They didn't have to answer, he could tell it was so.

"You go back to town," he said. "Find your sister. She needs you. I say that five will get you ten Rowayton's not far from her." He'd taken cartridges from his belt and was reloading the Colt. "Tell her what happened, and tell her I'll be back."

With a nod he turned Duke and kicked him once, starting him into a canter down the trail.

TWENTY-FOUR

Clem Hollinger was waiting for him when he rode up. The Gunsmith was grinning.

"We'll get on up to Six Mile Canyon now and take a look-see," the Gunsmith said. "Holbrook says you know the way."

"Been there a number of years back, but I still remember it."

They rode in silence for a long time, halting to rest and water the horses around noon then pressing on, though Clint was carefully checking their back trail now.

"You think those two fellers will keep their mouths shut?" Clem Hollinger asked.

"They should. But with humans you never know."

It was around the middle of the afternoon when Hollinger said, "Up there, I'm pretty damn sure that's it. Up yonder. There's a ravine with a sandy bottom just before we start up toward where his mine ought to be."

There was still a good bit of daylight when they found the ravine. The Gunsmith let Hollinger lead the way up a wide path that had once handled wagons but now was just a trail.

"We'd better come in from over there," Clint said. "They could easily be watching."

"Oh, sure," Hollinger agreed. "We can slip around that big stand of rock and come up above the mine. I just hope it's the right one—the one you got in mind."

They rode for another twenty minutes, moving up higher until they rounded a knoll. Hollinger drew rein and Clint pulled up beside him. They were looking down at the mine.

"Yep," Hollinger said, scratching one of his knobby elbows. "That's the old stamp mill Hank Towne worked. I heard it that he'd hit a vein that began paying off at a rate of eight hundred dollars a ton of ore. Hank thought he'd struck a lode that would make the Comstock look pretty sick, so the story goes; so he financed his own mill and reduction plant, only to have the vein peter out about as soon as he'd fired up his boilers. Went flat busted broke and sold out to Rowayton. Rowayton sunk a new shaft going down another thirty feet, made a crosscut thirty feet long, and claimed he hit that vein again. Mine's been paying off real good, according to everyone I hear tell it."

"Nothing appearing suspicious to anybody, huh?" Clint said.

"Well, Rowayton wouldn't let any of the other mining men take a look-see, but then nobody does. It's a matter of principle. Shit, now I understand he's producing six to eight bars of bullion a month. So Hercules Rowayton has just got to be in bonanza."

"You wait here," the Gunsmith said. "Keep your

eyes open. They've got outriders, not just the guards here at the mine. We could've been spotted coming in."

"Where you going?"

"I want to have a look. One's easier getting about than two."

The light was still strong, though the sun was getting close to the horizon as Clint slipped through the trees and brush that looked down on the mining camp.

He took his time as he circled around the lip of the canyon, taking in whatever detail was necessary. Mostly he was looking for other ways in or out of the camp. It seemed there was only the one trail in, which was being used at the present time. But he was interested in the mobility of anyone who would be defending the camp. Could help come in from another route, could there be an escape if needed? Was there a way someone not of the Rowayton camp could get in without being noticed? Also, how many men, how many horses? What did the guards' firepower appear to be? It seemed to the Gunsmith that Rowayton was keeping an extra heavy guard. More than would ordinarily be necessary. Why so many men, so heavily armed? He noted carefully the fine quality of horseflesh in the nearby patch of meadow and also in the round horse corral, where a dozen horses were ready for fast saddling and mounting.

Otherwise there seemed nothing out of the usual. There didn't seem to be very much activity, but perhaps it was just a moment where things were slacking off. Still, there were those gunmen. He didn't recognize any whom he might have seen on his visit to Rowayton's ranch on the Truckee. And he wondered again about Starch. Where had that somber figure disappeared to? What was his role in all of this play?

It was close to nightfall by the time he'd circled the ravine. Hollinger was right where he'd left him, and Clint was pleased to see how alert the older man was; waiting for him, in fact, with his gun out.

"Find what you wanted?" the Wells, Fargo man asked. "Anything special?"

The Gunsmith nodded, taking off his hat and wiping his forehead with his shirt-sleeve. "Got a pretty fair notion how it is."

"I see you're suspicioning something."

"They've got some guards down there," the Gunsmith said.

"Like all the mines." Hollinger spat briskly at a small bush. "Got to expect that, don't we."

"I reckon." The Gunsmith was canting his head at the evening sky.

"You see something?" Hollinger asked, suddenly more intent. "I mean, down in the mine."

Clint looked at him; a part of him still studying what he had noticed of the mining camp.

"Not what I saw so much, but what I felt."

"You got a hunch, is how it sounds," Hollinger said.

"That's the size of it. See, I didn't actually see anything any different from any mine."

"Then what?" The Wells, Fargo man was obviously puzzled.

"Each separate thing was just fine. The horses, the guns, the men, the layout. There's a trail out by that big rock yonder, but that's nothing special. Didn't see any tracks there."

"Then what?" Hollinger asked again.

"It's not the separate parts, but the feel of the whole that's interesting."

"Huh?"

"See, they've got guards, like I said. But why so many, so heavily armed? And why those horses? You don't need that quality of fast horseflesh for digging in a mine, do you?" He scratched the side of his chin. "The whole feel of the place just isn't right. And I'm beginning to get a suspicion why."

He said no more, and Hollinger had the good sense not to press.

It was dark when the mounted their horses and rode as quickly as they could away from Six Mile Canyon.

TWENTY-FIVE

"So your hunch tells you something's funny up there at Six Mile Canyon." Holbrook regarded the Gunsmith with his one good eye, leaning his elbows on his desk and fidgeting with one of his wanted posters.

"I know there is," Clint said. "I've checked around at a number of the other mines, and this one's special."

"So what does that prove? Nothing."

"I'm not trying to prove anything. I'm just looking to see which way to go," the Gunsmith said, and he squinted at the man behind the cluttered desk. "You did hire me to help you, didn't you?"

Holbrook's long face suddenly broke into a grin. "That's for sure," he said, and laughed. "Tell me what you're suggesting, Clint."

"I figure they're getting ready for something. The place had that kind of feel to it."

"Uh-huh."

"I've talked to some mining people around town. I know something about mining myself. And I'll bet my last dollar they're not mining a damn thing up there at Six Mile Canyon."

"What do you figure they're doing then?"

"I don't know, except to ask how the road agents who have stolen so much bullion here on the Comstock alone are getting rid of it—all that gold and silver in bars with a name stamped on it. How else but by melting it all down, eliminating the brand names, and then—"

"And then 'mine' it at the Six Mile!" Holbrook cut in fast. He shook his head in disbelief. "Pretty obvious, huh?"

"Sure. It's simple. It's a perfect cover."

"But how can you prove it?" Holbrook said suddenly. "You can't get anywhere near the place. You walk into that place, you're trespassing." He sniffed, drumming the fingers of both hands on the papers on his desk. "We have to obey the law. That's the goddamn problem, ain't it!"

"For you," the Gunsmith said.

"And for you, by God!" barked Holbrook. "You're working for Wells, Fargo, and you go by the law. Well, as much as you can," he added lamely.

The Gunsmith smiled. "I'm your advisor. I don't work for anybody, Holbrook." Clint's tone was quite friendly, and also quite firm.

The Wells, Fargo man nodded. "You're dealing."

"Good. Now then, as we've said, holding up a stagecoach is not the same as holding up an express car."

"An express car forted up with enough to repel a small army," said Holbrook. "I'd say it was impossible."

"To hold up a locked and barred express car—yes,

I agree,'' the Gunsmith said. ''But there is still a way.''

''You tell me how then.''

''Simple. Think like whoever it is behind the road agents. Rowayton? How would he do it? He'd likely hold up the whole train instead of only the express car. That's what I'd do. If you could take over the locomotive, you could pull the train onto a siding, leaving the main track clear. Then, if the express clerk and guard refuse to open the door, you blow up the express car with dynamite. The rest is a matter of transportation.''

''Jesus . . .'' Holbrook murmured. ''Jesus Christ, all I can say is I'm glad you're working with us, and not against us, my friend.''

''I'm not finished.'' There was the suspicion of a smile on Clint's face as he watched Holbrook's reactions.

''Go ahead.'' The agent leaned back in his chair, lifting his arms to lace his fingers together behind his head. He kept his good eye hard on the Gunsmith as he listened.

''Here's what we need to do. However they want to pull it off with the big job that's coming up—''

''You mean, the treasure train,'' Holbrook interrupted.

''Right. I want that information to get out to them.''

''Shit.''

''They probably know about it already.''

''I dunno about that.''

''Then make sure it gets to them. I want them to hold up that train—derail it, steal it, whatever.''

"But that train's going to have the biggest shipment of ore ever," said Holbrook, in alarm now. "You're asking something crazy, Clint! I can't do that. Allow a robbery!"

"After they get the loot they'll head for the mine. At least that's what I figure they'll do. Listen, Holbrook, you want to catch them in the act. Sure, you can whip up a hot posse and gun down some road agents. But you want a real killing so they're wiped out once and for all. Right?"

"Sure I want a killing—a real ending to it. This has got to be something that will be heard throughout the country. A warning that we mean business. But it has got to be legal."

"That's why I'm telling you to do it my way. You want to catch them redhanded in their operation at the mine. You want to get in there and see what's going on. It's a risk, mind you, because my hunch could be wrong." He paused and then added, "Except I know it isn't. But you want evidence for the courts. This is a big operation. Someone—and we suspect Rowayton—is making a mountain of gold!"

"Couldn't we run a fake shipment through?"

"It's got to be the real thing. They've got to see the actual ore. Feel it, dream about it! If they see it's fake, they'll be on guard."

"Sure, sure. I know. So what you're saying is you want Wells, Fargo to let them take that express car, letting them think it's an easy job, and now they're all richer than a top whore after six dozen Saturday nights."

"You got it." The Gunsmith grinned at the man at the desk.

"And we follow them."

"Wrong!"

"We're already out at the mine."

"Right!"

"Holy shit!"

"While you're arranging all that, I'll be working at something else."

The Gunsmith had started toward the door of the office.

"Like what?" Holbrook's words caught him with his hand on the doorknob.

"It might be a good idea to see if we can distract our friend's mind just at this time," he said.

"Yeah? What do you have in mind?"

The Gunsmith was grinning. "I'm going to try it the best way there is; the only way."

He closed the door quickly behind him, grinning as he thought of Sandra Lee Dorrance and her very jealous gentleman friend.

TWENTY-SIX

It was a six-handed game in the back room at the Antelope, and everybody put in a dollar, making it a six-dollar pot. The Gunsmith spotted the girl right away. She wasn't moving, just watching, quite still, her dark eyes not missing a thing. The only movement she made was to lift the cigar from the edge of the table, place it between her lips and draw. Clint hadn't known that Sandra Lee was a cigar smoker, but he wasn't surprised. Not a few of the few women gamblers favored that sort of tobacco, and some favored the booze too. He didn't know if the lady watching the game was of the latter persuasion, but she didn't look like a drinker.

Then Clint spotted the cold-decker. Until that moment his eyes had been completely taken by Sandra Lee and the big panatela in her mouth. She was gorgeous.

The cold-decker was wearing a brilliant red satin vest with flowers patterned on it in gold. His shirt was white. He wore a light gray derby.

The Gunsmith had no wish to play poker, but he'd felt the need for a drink while collecting his thoughts on how to approach Sandra Lee Dorrance without Hercules Rowayton finding out about it. Not an easy task since the hulk following her was in clear evidence and didn't mind anybody knowing it. He was, of course, showing himself under Rowayton's orders.

The cold-decker was really trimming the suckers, and Clint caught the sparkle in Sandra Lee's eyes as she watched the game. She looked at him briefly, but gave no sign of recognition. A true lady of the cards.

After ruminating on the situation awhile Clint had an idea. The next time a player vacated a seat, he moved into the game.

The dealer was clean shaven, with round, gray-colored cheeks, and heavy circles beneath his eyes. Clint noted that he'd been doing all right shaving the suckers, and would now try to add to his winnings by including the newcomer. Sandra Lee had still not joined the game, but the Gunsmith noted how the men left a good space for her to watch, treating her with cool respect.

"Like to join in, would you?" the cold-decker asked her as he riffled the cards.

The Gunsmith heard the contempt in Sandra Lee's voice as she said, "No thank you. I prefer to watch." And he knew she could have taken the dealer to the bank and back in a half-dozen hands.

His name was Cooley, and he continued to deal. The man on his left opened with a four showing. The next man raised on a queen. Clint had a six showing and he stayed; he was holding a king in the hole. Cooley dealt himself an ace. On the next time around Clint caught another six, and then a second king. Everyone had dropped out by now except Cooley, who had two aces and a trey showing.

His small eyes glistened under the gaslight as he said, "Let's sweeten 'er a little." And he suddenly pushed four hundred in chips into the middle of the table.

The Gunsmith was certain now that he was using a sleeve holdout. He checked his own hand and saw he didn't have the cards to go against whatever Cooley was going to deal himself. He knew for sure he wasn't going to get anything good. Well, he could fold or he could stay in and flush the sonofabitch. Cooley didn't even know how to use his holdout professionally. He was a real dummy, and bad for the game. At the same time Clint didn't want to make trouble with Sandra Lee there. He'd entered the game only in order to get to talk with her. But she clearly didn't want to socialize. She sat there staring in disgust at the cold-decker and his shenanigans. Yet inept as he was, he was fooling all the others at the table.

Clint felt he had to do something, and maybe this was the way to get to her. "I'll see you," he said, and pushed his money out toward the pot.

He was waiting, his eyes soft so they could see quickly; his body like a spring, ready. He was watching for the giveaway, the movement that would tell him Cooley was using a holdout.

There was a fair crowd standing around the table, mostly because of Sandra Lee. Several men had asked if she was to play that evening, but to one and all she remained impassively silent, or else murmured a "No thank you."

It was a sizable pot. "Must be a couple of thousand dollars in that pot," somebody said.

Cooley grinned and ran his tongue along his upper lip. Clint noted that he was minus a few teeth.

"Glad to have you stickin' with me, mister," Cooley said, and he shrugged, once, and again.

The Gunsmith knew that the next card Cooley dealt him would be a king or a six. He'd revealed his giveaway.

"Luck," Cooley said as he dealt the Gunsmith a third six. With a king showing and another king in the hole, he had a full house, good enough for a strong bet. Cooley, of course, was counting on it. He would deal himself a third ace—the fourth was already in the hole.

"Let 'er rip," somebody in the crowd said. "Bet 'em and play 'em!"

The Gunsmith had already shifted in his chair so that he'd be loose and ready to go in any direction.

Cooley shrugged his shoulders twice and dropped his hand to the deck to deal the final card.

Swift as smoke the Gunsmith reached across the green baize tabletop and grabbed the dealer by the wrist. With his other hand he reached into the man's sleeve and pulled the holdout right onto the discards.

"You sonofabitch!" Cooley screamed, jumping to his feet.

The Gunsmith slammed Cooley's hand down hard on the table and grabbed the fourth ace that fell out of his sleeve.

The dealer's right hand streaked to his coat. But quicker than light the Gunsmith stabbed his two hard fingers right into the other man's eyes, momentarily blinding him. Cooley screamed with pain and fell back. But he was tough. He suddenly recovered and lunged forward, striking at the Gunsmith, who kicked him once in the crotch. It was enough.

At that moment a shotgun blast ripped through the room. The Gunsmith turned to see Marshal Hank Doanes standing in the doorway that led to the rear of the saloon. He held a sawed-off twelve-gauge shotgun in his hands.

"That will do it! Or the next load will buy a few of you a six-by!"

The fight was over anyway. Cooley lay gasping in agony on the floor, his face contorted, trying vainly to curse but in too much pain to be articulate. The cards and money lay scattered all over the floor.

"Marshal," the Gunsmith said. "The man was using a holdout and I called him. Sorry about the damage."

Marshal Doanes, who was famous for minding his own business rather than the law, nodded and lowered his shotgun. "Just don't want this place wrecked," he said, cutting his eyes toward the bar. "I'll take a whiskey." As he moved toward the bar he nodded agreeably to Sandra Lee. "Ma'am . . ."

Sandra Lee acknowledged the marshal's greeting in silence. Then she walked to a nearby cuspidor and dropped her cigar into it.

Suddenly her eyes were directly on the Gunsmith, who'd been watching her move. "That's a good bit of money on the floor."

"It'll pay for the damage," the Gunsmith said, and he watched Cooley struggling to his feet as the saloon swept back to normal.

"I'll see you again, mister!" The threat was muttered through his struggle with pain.

"No you won't, Cooley," the Gunsmith said. "You'll stay out of my way. Make no mistake about that!"

He was quick enough to catch the sparkle in the girl's eyes as she heard him.

"I'd like to escort you wherever you wish to go, ma'am," he said.

She said nothing as he accompanied her out of the saloon.

TWENTY-SEVEN

They walked along the street toward her house mostly in silence. Clint was aware of their being followed, and wondered if Sandra Lee knew it.

As they came within sight of where she lived she finally spoke. "I would like to invite you in, Mr. Adams, for some refreshment, but I'm afraid there's a man following us, or at any rate, following me."

"I think we could arrange to get around that," Clint said as they stopped in front of her door. "I can be back in a very short while, if you'd like some company."

She was looking right into his eyes, and he could see that the excitement of the poker game and fight was still with her. Even as he'd been bracing the cold-decker he'd noticed the color in her cheeks, the way she was breathing, her breath catching sometimes, and her eyes sparkling, missing nothing.

"My, uh, house guest has her own part of the house, and so perhaps we can have a private conversation. I have some things I'd like to talk over with you."

Clint touched the brim of his hat and departed. He

walked quickly to the end of the street, turned the corner by the livery barn and waited.

It was only a few moments until the man came around the corner. The Gunsmith had his Colt out.

"You interested in what I'm going to be doing today?" he said, his voice cold as a new deck of cards.

"I dunno what yer talking about," the man said. "Look, I want nothin' to do with you, mister."

"You seemed interested in the poker game, and you were interested enough to follow me down the street. And here you are still. Now get! Get your ass out of my sight. And keep it that way. Just remember this gun is loaded!"

The man was not long on foolhardiness, or courage. He'd paled considerably and his legs were not too steady as he turned away and hurried back along the street.

"Run!" called the Gunsmith, and snapped a shot near the man's feet.

The owlhooter began running, and Clint cut two more bullets in close to speed him on his way. Then, satisfied, he reloaded, dropped his gun back into its holster, and walked quickly back up to the residence of Mrs. Sandra Lee Dorrance. He hoped he wouldn't run into Sally Miller, for he still had her on his mind—and in his pants, he told himself with a smile. But a bird or bush in the hand was worth two in the thoughts.

Sandra Lee had changed into a flowing housedress with an open neckline and revealing folds and contours, accented by what was inside.

"I can offer you coffee, Mr. Adams. Or would

you prefer something stronger? I have some very fine brandy.''

"Brandy would be fine, Mrs. Dorrance."

"Sandra Lee."

"Clint."

They shared a laugh at the exchange, and soon were seated and facing each other across a low table on which she'd placed their drinks.

"Sally has gone to bed."

He said nothing, but sat admiring the clear curve of her breasts as they pushed at her dress.

"You said you wanted to talk to me about something."

"Yes." There was a little smile at the corners of her mouth.

"What? The weather?"

Suddenly a small laugh burst from her. "How did you know? You must be a mind reader, knowing I had that question burning at me for several days now.''

He grinned. "Funny coincidence."

"It is, isn't it."

"I mean, I have a burning question also."

"Do you?"

He put down his drink and moved quickly around the little table to sit beside her on the settee.

"Yes," he said, taking her hand and kissing it. "Do you think you could help me?"

Her breath caught and her cheeks flushed as he very lightly began caressing her breasts. "Yes, Mr. Adams. I mean Clint. I'll try. But let's go inside."

In moments they were in her bedroom with the door locked. He was already undressing her. Her dress fell smoothly to the floor and in a moment her firm, bouncing breasts burst into his hands. The nipples were big, hard, red. Bending his head, he took one in his mouth, biting it a little as she gave a quiet squeal of delight.

Meanwhile she had his organ out of his pants, and gripping it firmly, led him to the bed. In the next moment they were totally naked and he mounted her easily, her slit soaking wet and easing the passage of his cock. He began stroking her slowly as her buttocks moved in tune with his, and she began to moan into his ear.

He didn't rush it, though he could tell she was anxious for a climax. He took his time, teasing, delaying, letting it build to that impossible mania before exploding, And now they were going faster, her hips, loins, legs—everything in perfect timing with him until neither could stand even another split second and they came exactly together, squirming into submission to their total passion, finally subsiding into the soft wide bed with their arms and legs still wrapped around each other.

"My God, you do that even better than you play poker."

"So do you," he said, and added, "Actually, though, now that I look into that question, I'm not so sure you do it better than you play poker."

"Oh?" She sat up on her elbow and looked down at him, one marvelous boob jouncing right into his face. His lips took her nipple and he continued to speak to her as he teased it.

Then she said, "Do you really believe that I can't make love better than I can play poker? I can, you know."

He let go of her nipple. "Prove it."

After the third time around she said, "Well?"

"Well what?" He was feeling sleepy.

"Have I answered your question?"

He smiled up at the ceiling. "You sure have."

She was up on her elbow again, this time with her other boob bouncing down into his face. "You know something?"

"What?"

"I'm not really sure myself whether I play cards better."

"Aren't you ever satisfied?" he said as he felt his organ beginning to grow.

TWENTY-EIGHT

Luckily it was dark when he took his departure and walked back to the Boston House. Vaguely he wondered if Sally Miller had been awake while he'd been visiting her landlady. He had heard nothing, and in fact had been too fully occupied to be concerned whether she'd been aware of his presence. There wasn't any way she would have known it was him, he concluded, and wondered why that concerned him. But of course, it didn't, he told himself, except insofar as he hoped to share her bed in the not distant future. But not in the same house. He knew the Sandra Lee type all too well. She was exactly like Rowayton, a monument to self-esteem. Jealousy incarnate. And it was this thought that stopped him in the lobby of the Boston House.

Sure, there'd been no one about when he'd left the girl. Sure. His eyes went to the desk where the clerk sat dozing.

"Wake up and keep your mouth shut," he said, pointing the Colt right at the man's head.

The amazed clerk—a young man hardly in his twenties—almost started to stammer as he looked into that hard round hole and then up at the two

157

bullet eyes of the Gunsmith.

"Y-yes, I mean n-no, sir."

"Do I have visitors?"

The young man was speechless. He could only nod.

"Where?"

The room clerk's eyes moved upward toward the stairs to the landing above.

"How many?"

"Three."

He'd dropped the Colt back into its holster when he heard the sound behind him. He stepped clear of the desk and in one flowing movement dropped down on his back, rolled, drew and fired at the man behind him. One shot. The man who'd tried to kill him was as dead as the silence that filled the lobby of the Boston House.

"Mister . . . m-mister . . ." The clerk was ready to faint. "I di-di-didn't know. I . . . I . . ."

"Consider yourself lucky that I believe you."

There was a rush of feet on the landing above, and steps coming down the stairs. But they stopped, waited. He could see only legs.

"Come on down, gentlemen, unless you want your legs shot off. Come down!" The last words were snapped out.

The three men were a sad-looking crew. Their hands were up; they were done for.

"Drop your guns back of the desk there and get out!"

They moved quickly then, stepping over their dead companion, who was lying facedown in a pool of blood.

"One of you send the marshal," the Gunsmith said. "And I don't want to see a one of you within ten miles of me. Now get!"

He holstered the six-gun and turned back to the young man behind the desk, who was as white as his shirt.

"I don't know if they'll get hold of Doanes at this hour, or even if the sonsofbitches will try, but I want some sleep. I'll be back in the morning."

Without another look at the dead man, the Gunsmith turned on his heel and walked out of the back door of the Boston House. It was still dark as he walked down to the livery. He'd sleep down in the stall with Duke. Hell, he'd slept with his old friend more than a few times, and he knew that if anyone approached him who shouldn't, Duke would know it and let him know in plenty of time.

The Gunsmith was tired. He'd had a full night— the card game, the fun with Sandra Lee, and the action at the Boston House. Who the hell was it ever spoke of taming the West? he asked himself.

Satiated as he had certainly been after his tryst with Sandra Lee, the Gunsmith found himself with Sally Miller still on his mind. For one thing, he'd been wondering what had happened to her brothers after he had backwatered Tom and, he hoped, taught him a lesson. Had the lesson taken hold? Had he learned something? Had Dave helped him through the humiliation? Or had Tom decided to go renegade? The Gunsmith knew all too well that such events could turn out badly. He'd tried to teach the damn fool kid something, but had the damn fool kid learned? And had they gone to find their sister?

His thoughts of Sally Miller were on a different level. He found his passion mounting at just the thought of her, without any sexual description in his mind. Just her name, the color of her hair, the vision of how she moved was enough to excite him.

She was definitely on his mind the next morning as he left the Wells, Fargo office after checking plans with Warner Holbrook. Things were coming to a head. The express car would soon be loaded and on its way to San Francisco. Guards were preparing for the trip—some of Wells, Fargo's top men. And the secret treasure train had been bruited about every saloon and bedroom on the Comstock. The road agents were finished, so the news went; they hadn't a chance going up against an armored express car. The stories multiplied along with the number of guards who would be riding shotgun. Also multiplied well beyond the wildest realm of possibility was the amount of the treasure. But people loved to talk.

Actually the plan was simple. After going over it carefully with the Gunsmith, Holbrook had allowed the news to be spread through channels that would be sure to reach the waiting ears of the road agents. They would know that the treasure train was indeed going to roll; and it was said along with this news that only a few guards—one, two, maybe three—would be in attendance. After all, how necessary was it to protect a fortress? You could only do so much up to a point, and then extra people made for confusion.

The Gunsmith had insisted on certain points, and Holbrook—his fingers fidgeting more than ever—had seen the sense in agreeing with him. He'd never seen Clint Adams in action, but he'd gotten a first-hand account from the Boston House room clerk of the doings in the lobby when the Gunsmith outdrew and outshot a man who had the drop on him from the rear.

Leaving Holbrook, Clint felt the satisfaction of a

man who had done all he could possibly do in a given situation, and now it was time to roll 'em or get out of the game. Walking back to the Boston House he felt just right, with the warm sun beating down on the backs of his hands and on his shoulders and arms. The one problem that faced him now was how he would get to see Sally Miller without Sandra Lee knowing about it. Well, he'd find a way, by God. He already had the will for it. The rest would turn up. And it did.

The expression on the room clerk's face told him something had happened. It was the same doughy-looking youth of the night before.

"More visitors?" Clint asked, eyeing the young man coldly.

"No sir, Mister Adams. It's a . . . a lady." He nodded toward the dining room.

Clint's spirits soared as he stepped across the lounge and entered the large room. She was at the same table, again with a book. But she looked up immediately—and—by golly!—smiled at him.

"You sure surprised me, Sally. I was thinking about you."

He sat down, removed his hat, and let his eyes rest on her, studying her to see how she was.

"Have you found anything out? I went to see Marshal Doanes again and he was no help at all."

"I do have news."

"Oh, tell me!" She leaned forward, grabbing him by the wrist, her eyes wide with yearning for even a crumb of information.

"I saw them. I spoke with them. But I didn't come to you right away because I wanted it to be their move."

"Oh, tell me everything!"

First he made her promise that she would wait and not do anything foolish in the way of looking them up on her own; that she would wait to let them come to her, and if they didn't, would consult with him before she took any action. When she'd agreed, he told her about them following him and how he'd confronted them, but left out any details that put Tom in a truly bad light.

"Oh, Clint . . ." She was dabbing at her eyes with her handkerchief. "I don't care what they've done. I mean, I just want to see them. Will you tell them? Will you tell them you've spoken with me and I want them? I don't care what they've been doing. I won't question them. And tell them that nothing I know or hear about them will go any further. Please tell them to come. I'll go to meet them anywhere they like."

They talked for a while longer, until she'd calmed down. And again he walked her to the door of the Boston House, as he had at their last encounter.

They stood for a few moments on the narrow front porch. For just those moments it seemed quieter in the street. The crowd wasn't there, and Clint felt her presence with him all the more. He could actually feel the emanations of her warmth, her sex. At one point he even held her eyes with his as his passion grew, spreading. He had to fight the urge to take her in his arms.

"Will you please tell Tom and Dave?" she said.

"I will."

"I . . . I like you," she said, and her cheeks colored as she turned and walked quickly away.

TWENTY-NINE

"All right, then, you understand what you have to do." Hercules Rowayton stood in front of his roll-top desk, the four fingers of both hands pushed into the tops of his trousers. His broad shoulders were slightly hunched, his handsome face tight and pale with barely suppressed anger. His was a cold anger, actually beyond heat.

The man in the black suit, standing in front of him, stared impassively at him. "Don't worry."

"I'm not worried! I'm simply making sure that you understand what you're about to do."

"I am going to kill him, that's what I'm gonna do," Starch said.

"You're going to kill him in front of witnesses. You'll show the town, the West, the whole damn world that you're the top gunfighter!"

There was not the slightest sign of emotion in the other man's face as he listened to Rowayton. "But I already am the top gunfighter!"

"I know, I know." Rowayton held up a placating palm. "I know you are. But the world doesn't know it. You've got to prove it."

"I don't have to prove nothin'," Starch insisted. "But I am aimin' to kill the sonofabitch anyways."

"Have it your own way. But the killing, the actual killing, has to be my way."

"Huh!"

"You draw, you shoot, you kill. But I will set it up and I—*I*—will let you know the right moment. Is that understood."

"Huh . . ."

"Starch!"

"Yeah."

"First we get the gold shipment. It'll be immediately after. I'll let you know. You stay out of sight. Maybe let him see you once or twice—no more than that."

He looked at Starch for a long moment. Starch said nothing.

"You understand—you wait for my signal."

Starch nodded.

When Starch had left, Rowayton quickly poured himself a drink. By God, he'd show her. He would show that damn bitch! He would show her who was top gun in the country!

He was brooding over his drink, torturing himself with his raging jealousy right up until the time Billie and Callie knocked at his door.

Thank God for this, he was thinking as the two of them went to work on his penis and balls. It certainly took his mind off that damn bitch! Yet it was Sandra Lee who was in his thoughts as they played for the longest time. There were moments when he forgot her, forgot what terrible thing she had done to him; but only for a moment. She was there. Sandra Lee with those superb tits and that exquisite ass . . . Hercules didn't even know which of the two girls he came inside of, for it was the gorgeous Sandra Lee who claimed him.

"So when are we gonna tell her?"

"I keep telling you—when this job is done."

"Tom, it's going on forever. Sal might not wait all that long."

"She'll wait."

"You know what? I saw her. I saw her walking down the street."

"You damn fool! Did she see you?"

"Tom, don't you figure that Gunsmith told her what happened?"

"I don't care if the sonfofabitch did. I'm not going to tell her, and you better not. The sonfofabitch tricked me. But he won't get away with that next time."

"Tom, for God sakes, give up on it. He beat you fair and square. He was greased lightning. I never seen anything move that fast."

"Bullshit!"

They were sitting on the top bar of the round horse corral at the Four Aces. It was evening, yellow light slanting low across the land. Dave Miller was chewing, and Tom had a stem of bunch grass hanging from his mouth.

"I hope he didn't tell her," Dave said.

"I told you, I don't give a shit."

"You heard about the gold train."

"Who the hell hasn't."

"Think Stash is gonna take it on?"

"How's his leg is the thing. He was limping."

"Stash is a tough one."

"That Starch sonofabitch is tough. But he ain't all that tough. He could be useful when we work over the train."

"You mean, the express car."

"That's the important part of the train. It'll be jammed full with you know what. I'd like to get my hands on some of that!"

"We'll get paid."

"Paid! Shit!" Tom spat at a pile of fresh horse manure, hitting it plumb center.

"After, Tom. After the express car we'll look up Sal. Right?"

"Depends."

"But Tom, you promised."

"I promised nothing exceptin' I'm going to get that Gunsmith and show him. Who the hell does that bastard think he is! Pulling that smartass stuff on us. Like I was a damn kid or something."

"Compared to him, we're kids. Can't you see that?"

"Shut up!"

Dave spat out a mouthful of tobacco. "Tell you what. I'm going to look up Sal when this is over, when we've pulled the express-car job. And you can do what you like." He dropped down from the corral pole where he'd been sitting near his brother and started walking toward the bunkhouse.

Tom Miller watched him go. He felt a choking in his throat, and was too angry to say anything.

THIRTY

The plan had been thought out most carefully by Hercules Rowayton. It had been clear to him from the start that the only way to achieve success was to hold up the entire train. It was an historic moment, the end of an era in stage robbing and the beginning of a new era in train robbery. Everything appeared to be going according to plan.

The wood-burning engine dragged the train out of the station and gathered speed on its way to deliver the contents of the special express car—the Treasure Car.

Led by Big William and Dutch Wagner, the main body of the road-agent gang were waiting in a town called Oak Crossing, where the train was to stop, refuel, and take on water. Earlier they had traveled a mile down the track and transferred a pile of railroad ties to the rails. They did a good job under Big William's supervision, putting one tie across the rails, then a row across it, parallel to the rails, with the butt ends of these ties braced against cross ties and the top ends facing any oncoming train. The result was a stack over four feet high.

Pleased with the result of their activity, the boys retired to Oak Crossing to relax and wait for the train. The little town, just inside the Nevada line from California, was as new as the railroad that ran through it. It existed for one reason only—it was the closest point on the Central Pacific to the big lumber camps up around Loyalton and Sierraville. The town was already dwarfed by mountainous piles of timbers; some of the logs were sixty feet long and as much as six and seven feet thick. These were to be shipped to the mines. It also sported the usual skid road over which the logs were skidded; along the road were the customary saloons, hotels, restaurants, stables, and other necessaries. The eager road agents waited in one of the places of pleasure.

Presently the train was heard and the boys were off. The train came bustling around the bend, its big oil lamp gleaming into the night, sparks were thrown out of its funnel. The brakes grabbed and the train jerked to a crashing halt, ready to refuel and take on water.

Dutch Wagner, Big William, and their boys watched quietly from the big stacks of mine timber. All wore black masks.

After a wait, the brakeman waved a lantern, the engine belched out an incredible eruption through its funnel, and the train started with a massive jerk. As the express car rolled past them, Dutch and his companions swung up onto the steps of the passenger car behind it. Inside the train two more Rowayton men, masquerading as passengers, started to move casually toward the express car. They were there as backup men, in case they were needed.

Dutch Wagner and his men, swinging aboard, were

met by a brakeman who was just getting ready to enter the coach. He gave a startled call and grabbed for the door catch. Stash Hammond had him in an instant and rushed him across the platform. For an instant it looked as though both of them would go over the side, but it was the brakeman alone who landed beside the track.

Dutch and Stash began immediately climbing to the top of the express car, with Big William and two other men supporting them over the swaying, jolting gap between the cars. Dutch and Stash made their way over the top of the express car to the tender, which was piled high with wood for the firebox. It was tricky climbing over the wood, but they made it. They dropped suddenly into the cab, drawing their guns, terrifying the fireman and engineer. Dutch was following orders to the letter.

About a mile and a half south of Oak Crossing, on a level stretch of track, Dutch ordered the engineer to stop the train. This signaled one of the gang to set the brake on the passenger cars and pull the coupling pin linking them to the express car. It all went off like clockwork.

When he got the signal that the cars were separated, Dutch ordered the engineer to get the engine and express car moving. Peering ahead in the moonlight, Dutch saw the switch that cut the spur into the main line and told the engineer to stop the train. Stash jumped down, along with Big William, and together they threw the switch, according to plan. The locomotive chugged into the spur and stopped a couple of hundred yards away from the main track.

"Hell, man, you can't leave those passenger cars sitting back there on the track," the engineer protested to Dutch Wagner. "There's a fast freight due along in twenty minutes."

"Don't worry," Dutch told him. "The freight can't leave where it's at until you pull in. And besides, we've got the track blocked. So shut up and just do what I tell you."

By now Stash Hammond and his men had started pounding on the express-car door.

"Who is it?" shouted the express car clerk. He sounded alarmed, for indeed the train's stopping had made him very suspicious.

"It's all right," Dutch called back as he came up to meet Stash and the other men. "Open up, I'm from Wells, Fargo—special agent Holbrook."

Just then—as the Gunsmith pointed out later to Holbrook and Hollinger as they reworked the holdup in the Wells, Fargo office—the bandits blew their chances. No express car clerk in his right mind would have opened up on such flimsy evidence. The fact that the clerk did should have tipped off the bandits that they were walking into a trap.

The door was opened just slightly. Immediately hands grabbed it and forced it back. The road agents poured in.

Two kerosene lamps suspended from the ceiling of the express car illuminated the scene within. At the front end was the mail compartment, separated from the express section by a wooden partition, in the center of which was a closed door. Behind the partition the mail clerk was moving around. The bandits could hear him.

But the road agents weren't interested in the U.S. Mail. The express box filled with gold was in the center of the car.

There was a fire axe on the wall of the car. Big William grabbed it and split the box open. A storm of gold coins flew around the car, landing on the floor. All the other boxes in the car were opened in a similar manner. Only one had money in it; it contained ten thousand silver dollars.

Barking orders to his men, Dutch Wagner backed the express clerk into a corner and knocked him out with the barrel of his six-gun. But the man squirmed as he landed on the floor, so Dutch shot him in the leg.

"That'll keep you still, you sonofabitch!"

Dutch and his men climbed out of the car, loaded with gold and silver. Standing at the side of the track by the engine, Dutch ordered the engineer to back out onto the mainline. The train began to move out slowly.

The waiting horses snorted and fussed, catching the excitement of the moment. Later, describing the scene to the Gunsmith, Holbrook, and Hollinger, the engineer remarked that he'd come within an ace of pulling the engine's steam whistle but had checked himself just in time. "Those horses would have been halfway to Mexico before the sound stopped," he'd said. "And that would have killed our plan for sure," added the Gunsmith with a smile.

The bandits waited until the locomotive had backed around the first bend and was out of sight. Dutch gave the order to mount and cut leather.

THIRTY-ONE

A bright moon gleamed in the sky as the Gunsmith, Clem Hollinger, and a band of selected men worked their horses along the steep, narrow trail that lead into Six Mile Canyon. It was unfortunate, Clint was thinking, for they needed all the help that was possible, such as good cover. They could well be outnumbered by the bandits. Moreover, the mine would be well guarded and there would be outriders. Clint held a hope that the men's confidence in Hercules Rowayton would make them careless, and that they'd believe the stories that Wells, Fargo thought the express car was impregnable and so they wouldn't need a lot of guards. Indeed, the ease with which they would take the express car would put them off guard.

Such was his hope. His plan was simple. They would simply ambush the returning party bringing the loot to the mine. One of the Wells, Fargo men aboard had a very fast horse in the baggage car. He would ride to tell them the news, hoping to get ahead of the victorious road agents on their triumphal return.

The posse, headed by the Gunsmith, reached the

entrance to the canyon around midnight. Clint ordered a dry camp, set out sentries, then mounted up again.

"I'll be back in a couple of hours likely," he told Hollinger. "Let the men rest, but keep sharp. They'll have outriders around the place."

"Got'cha. Clint, you take it careful. We need you."

"Just a little scouting," the Gunsmith said with a smile. "Keeps a man young."

"I hope it keeps you healthy," Clem Hollinger said sardonically, and both of them chuckled at that.

Clint had no trouble getting inside the mouth of the canyon. He picketed his horse in good cover, checked his weapons again—making sure his handgun came easily from its holster—and approached the mine on foot.

The moon was down, and while he could still see, he was more protected without its brilliance. Avoiding two sentries, he got quite close to the mine shaft. He noticed now that there was a light in the main shack, though the window was partially covered, and was glad to see that they were careless. He spent about an hour checking out the area, counting the horses in the corral, and figuring out how many men had to be on hand.

It was getting toward dawn when he got back to Hollinger and his band of men at the entrance to the canyon. The Wells, Fargo man who had been on the train had just ridden in on a near foundering horse. "They're on their way with the money. They're not far back of me."

"How many are they?" the Gunsmith asked.

"I figure a good two dozen, give or take."

"Shit," said Hollinger. "What do we do? If we ride in and take the mine now, they'll be jumping up our ass in no time. We're scissored, for Christ sake!"

"No, we're not." The Gunsmith turned back to the man who had brought the news. "Get a fresh horse. Clem, get the men mounted—right now! We're heading into the canyon, and we'll set up our ambush."

"For the bunch coming from the train?"

"That's it."

"But they'll *hear* the firing back at the mine. They'll hit us in the rear, what I was just saying!"

"No they won't. You're going to take six men and attack the mine. You'll hold them. Don't move in unless there's an excellent chance—if you really catch them short. But probably the best thing will be to hold them while we'll take on the train bunch. Get moving!" He snapped the last words at the amazed Hollinger and then was up on Duke and signaling the men to follow him.

The whole bunch dashed to the place the Gunsmith had found while he was scouting—where the trail into the canyon narrowed between high rocks. Perfect for an ambush.

There was no time to be lost. Swiftly he placed the men, giving them strict orders not to shoot or make a sound until he fired or ordered them. Then he dispatched Hollinger and his men.

"You wait there until you here us firing, then open up. Now, there's a sentry on each side of the trail as you ride in, just before you round the knoll we passed when we rode in before; just before you come in sight of the shacks and the mine shaft.''

"I got it." Hollinger's grin spread all the way across his face.

"What are you grinning about?" the Gunsmith asked.

"I like the way you work, Gunsmith."

"Mister, you might like it less if you don't remember not to call me that name again." He took the sting out of it by winking, but with no smile added. He liked Hollinger. "Get your ass moving," he snapped.

No sooner were they gone, the night swallowing them, than he heard the horses coming quickly into the canyon. They were making a lot of noise—confident, he thought, after the success of their night's work.

He wondered if Rowayton was with them. Probably not. But what about Wagner and Big William? And the boys? And Starch!

The Gunsmith had his men lined along both sides of the trail leading into Six Mile Canyon, some at ground level but most higher up in the rocks. It was now just getting to be dawn, and he could see the road-agent gang clearly. Big William and Dutch Wagner were in the lead, but there was no sign of the others he was looking for—the Miller boys, or Starch, or Rowayton, whom he really didn't expect to see.

Clint waited until the riders, slowing because of the narrow trail, had come about halfway down, with Hollinger's armed force covering them in front and behind.

"Halt!" he yelled out.

For a brief moment they didn't know what to

do—not from fear, but astonishment. Some reined their horses, others who didn't crashed into the riders ahead of them. There was cursing as they realized they could see no one to shoot it. The Gunsmith called out: "You men are trapped. Drop your guns and throw up your hands!"

A charged moment followed, and it ended with the crack of a rifle as one of the bandits shot in the direction he thought the voice had come from. His bullet sang into the rocks. Instantly there was the crash of multiple shooting, since the first shot had been a signal for the men to cut loose—both in Clint's ambush party and up ahead at the mine, with Clem Hollinger's force.

At the entrance to the canyon Big William fell with his horse, but landed with his gun blazing and managed to escape the crossfire. Men began to fall, tumbling from their horses as the withering fire from the rocks raked them. The bandits were now trying to make a fast retreat. Dutch Wagner had been shot but was clinging to his horse, which was out of control. He galloped right through his men, who were trying to escape while firing wildly at the rocks without seeing what they could shoot at. Suddenly Wagner straightened in his saddle, arching his back, then fell tumbling to the ground, shot through the spine.

Big William, meanwhile, had secured another horse and was racing toward the mine. Without a second's hesitation the Gunsmith swept into his saddle and kicked big Duke into a gallop. In moments the two horses had broken away from the battle and were racing toward the mine. Duke was gaining— there weren't any horses around who could beat him in a flat-out race. Big William was riding a big bay stallion, which was giving a good account of itself.

Suddenly the bay horse stumbled and his rider was thrown. Big William had gotten to his feet and was reaching for his six-gun by the time Clint was reining his horse. The Gunsmith knew he was in a bad position. His body was twisted in the saddle as he threw his weight into stopping Duke. Instead of trying to draw, he dropped out of the saddle, landing on his feet; hoping wildly that the other man would not shoot his horse.

"I got you, you sonofabitch!" screamed Big William, gun in his hand.

Maybe it was his excitement that got him, or maybe it was what everyone later said—that the Gunsmith was lightning in a greased sleeve. Clint drilled his man right between the eyes. Big William fell like a foundering buffalo under the impact of the bullet.

Without even looking at the fallen man, Clint was up on Duke again and galloping toward the mine. He could hear the gunfire slackening and wondered if it meant the fight was ending. He could hear no more gunfire behind him, and figured the bandits had been routed.

As he broke around the high knoll on the narrow trail he saw that Hollinger and his men were down in the mine area. There were two men lying in the dirt, four others facing Hollinger's men with their hands up.

When Clint rode up Hollinger said, "We lost a man, and another was wounded, but not bad."

Two riders now came pounding in, right on the Gunsmith's heels.

"We shot half a dozen," one of them said. "We

didn't get a full count, but they've took off—what was left of them.''

"The money?'' Hollinger asked.

"We've got it.''

"How many got away?'' Clint asked.

The man spat while reflecting, then said, "I reckon no more 'n' two, three.'' He turned to his companion, who was also breathing heavily from his swift ride.

"Two, three, I'd allow,'' said the other man.

"Good enough.'' The Gunsmith turned to Hollinger. "We'll ride back and check it all, and get the wounded back to the doc.'' He squinted up at the sun. "Fight didn't take so long as all that,'' he said. "We'll send men back with the wounded, but before you and me ride back I want to check out the mine. I know they been running their stolen bullion through the mill here, melting it down and putting their own brand on it.''

Hollinger looked puzzled. "How the hell did you figure that out?'' he asked.

The Gunsmith took off his Stetson hat and ran his shirt-sleeve over his forehead. Then he replaced his hat at a new angle. He squinted at the Wells, Fargo man.

"Wouldn't that be the way you'd do it?'' he said.

THIRTY-TWO

Warner Holbrook rubbed his knuckle into his blind eye to relieve an itch, leaned back in his swivel chair, and with his good eye surveyed the ceiling of his office.

"There's still Rowayton," he said. "And are we really sure it's him?"

"I don't think I could prove it in a court of law or before a judge," Clint said. "But it's him. No doubt about that."

"But we didn't catch him red-handed," Holbrook insisted.

"I didn't expect him to be on the scene. But I do figure on him making his move now. He's being pinched in more ways than one."

"How so?" Hollinger asked. He was sitting across the room on an upended crate; the Gunsmith was seated on the only other chair besides Holbrook's.

"He's had his gang busted," Clint said, "and his mine and stamp mill besides. And on top of that his girlfriend is giving him real trouble."

At this both Holbrook and Hollinger stared in surprise. "How the hell do you know that?" Holbrook asked suspiciously.

"A little bird told me."

The Gunsmith refused to say any more on that particular subject, though his two companions regarded him with expressions of surprise mixed with incredulity and amusement.

Holbrook cleared his throat. "So what happens now? Of course, we'll bring the gang to the law—not to Hank Doanes, but the circuit judge. That'll take time, and meanwhile they're in jail over at Reno. They should be safe there."

"And Rowayton?" Hollinger asked carefully, looking at Clint directly. "Do you think he'll take this lying down?"

The Gunsmith stood up. "I don't think so at all. In fact I'm counting on his not taking it lying down. Hercules Rowayton, I've been told, gentlemen, is a man who never takes no for an answer. He's been getting an awful lot of no's lately."

"Well, it's just yesterday things blew up for him," Holbrook said. "What do you reckon he's doing? I've got a man watching him. He hasn't left the country."

"He won't," the Gunsmith said.

"How can you be so sure?"

"That's easy," Clint said as he started toward the door. "He won't leave the country as long as I'm alive. And gentlemen, if I get suddenly dead—which I'm not planning on doing—then you can start to worry." With a nod and a smile to each of them, he walked out of the office.

It was noon, the sun high and hot in the tall sky. Yet the day seemed like any other. People were going about their business, the mule teams fighting their way in and out of town, the crowd still watching the stage depart from the Wells, Fargo depot, the saloons and gaming halls and whorehouses as active as ever.

And yet for the Gunsmith the day *did* feel different. For a moment he found himself thinking of the girl, Sally. He hadn't seen her in some time, and wondered if her brothers had contacted her. He hoped so. He hoped his backwatering Tom Miller wouldn't result in further trouble for that young man.

It was odd, he thought as he came back into the present, that the town seemed the same as always, yet at the same time, different. There was the same activity, yet underneath there was a current, as if people were waiting. He knew what they were waiting for, and so did those who'd been involved in the struggle with the road agents. Something had to be decided before much more time passed. Something had to be settled.

He found that he'd turned toward the Silver Dollar. Well, he thought, it was as good a place as any, since he was familiar with it. He knew the layout, the doors in and out; and he knew, too, as he approached the wooden building with the big sign on it, that this had to be the place where Rowayton would make his play. In the street there would be too many elements that could work against him. In the Silver Dollar the compact quarters would work to his advantage. The Gunsmith accepted that, for he knew from long experience that what could work for another man's advantage could also work for his.

The room was crowded, but not more so than usual. The first person he recognized, to his surprise, was Tom Miller, and then he saw his brother only a few feet away. Both were at the bar. He thought Dave gave a sign of recognition, but there was nothing coming from Tom. The older brother was wearing his holster tied down. Not a good sign at all, the Gunsmith thought. He'd been wondering how many he'd have to go up against, and had hoped that Tom Miller wouldn't be one of them. But it didn't look like it.

As he stood at the bar, facing the big mirror behind the rows of bottles, he noticed that behind him the room had suddenly grown quiet. Men were still attending to their drinking, their cards, their idle chatter. But something was muted now—there was a definite carefulness in the atmosphere. Three or four men put down their drinks, nodded to somebody, or maybe even to nobody, and took their leave of the premises.

The Gunsmith remained where he was, leaning lightly on the bar, watching the room in the mirror. He could see the bat-wing doors, the door to the back room, the steps leading to the balcony and the rooms where the girls plied their trade.

He was loose, and yet there was a necessary tension in his body, like the tension needed in a good spring. His thoughts were muted, that was the main thing— for he was attentive.

The Miller boys were standing at the other end of the bar, Tom nearest to him, Dave on the far side of his brother. He could come through the bat-wing doors, the Gunsmith was thinking, or the door to the rear of the saloon, or even the balcony—they could crossfire him. That would be the most likely, knowing Rowayton. But he was sorry to see Tom involved. He was really sorry for that. What other business would he have in the saloon?

Suddenly he heard Dave Miller. His words were indistinguishable, but he was saying something to his brother. Tom Miller's voice was clearer when he replied.

"They're setting you up, Adams." Clint felt the shock of his not calling him Gunsmith.

"That's what I figure, Tom." He was still leaning on the bar, but with no weight on it, and he was speaking to Tom in the mirror.

Tom Miller started to say something else but his voice was drowned out by the single word that reached Clint Adams through the low hum of the saloon, which abruptly became a dead silence.

"Gunsmith!"

He was coming down the stairs from the balcony —all black, black as the ace of spades, his face dead white around his black eyes and the black circles beneath them, his black stovepipe hat square on his head.

"Howdy, Starch! I missed you, my friend. Where you been all this time?"

"I'm going to kill you, Gunsmith."

He'd stopped a short distance from Clint, just at the bottom of the stairs, his arms down at his sides, his right hand with a black glove on it, the fingers twitching slightly.

"I got ten to one you'll bugger it, Starch."

"Gunsmith, you're finished."

"No, Starch. You are."

Never had the Gunsmith felt looser than at that moment as his hand—swifter than silence—swept to his sixgun.

In that split second he heeded Tom Miller's warning of just a moment before as he heard again "Gunsmith!" And there was Hercules Rowayton on the balcony.

Clint Adams had already shot Starch through the

throat, and as the man stood rock still for that dead second before falling, Clint threw his next shot at Rowayton and dropped to the floor.

Hercules Rowayton pulled the trigger of his gun just as he received the Gunsmith's bullet between his eyes. He was dead before the bullet he'd fired smashed the big mirror in back of the bar.

It was over.

An ash-white Tom Miller walked over to Clint Adams.

"Mr. Adams, I wouldn't go up against you if you gave me a million dollars!"

"Don't worry, Tom. If I ever did have a million, I wouldn't be giving it to you." He reloaded his gun while the saloon remained in frozen shock. Slipping his gun back into its holster he cut his eyes at Tom and Dave Miller. "On the other hand, Tom, I heard your warning. Maybe, in a way of speaking, you might say I owe you a million."

"You paid that, Mr. Adams," Tom said. "You paid!" And without another word he turned and followed his brother Dave out of the saloon.

Shortly, when the bodies had been removed and Warner Holbrook and Clem Hollinger walked into the Silver Dollar, they found the Gunsmith having a drink at the bar.

"Jesus," Warner Holbrook said. "You got two of them!"

"Looks like it," the Gunsmith said.

"That Starch was fast," Clem Hollinger observed.

"He isn't anymore," the Gunsmith said.

"But what's with Rowayton?" Holbrook asked, his astonishment still all over his face. "I never knew he went for guns. He never carried a gun. What the hell happened to the man!"

The Gunsmith put down his drink. "I don't know. But maybe I've got a notion on that, even so."

"Like what?" both men asked almost in unison.

"Like I suspicion he wanted to show his girlfriend he was the fastest gun in the West."

A good while later, after he'd had supper with Holbrook and Hollinger at the dining room in the Boston House, the Gunsmith found himself thinking about Sally Miller. He wanted to go and see her in the worst way, but he sure didn't want to run into Sandra Dorrance.

He spent the rest of the evening having a drink or two in one of the other saloons in town and came back early to the Boston House. As he walked into the lobby he saw the dough-faced boy behind the desk. There was definitely something wrong with him, and the Gunsmith was instantly on his guard.

"What's the matter with you?" he demanded.

"You . . . you got a visitor."

"What kind?"

"A lady."

"You let her upstairs? What the hell's the matter with you!" snapped the Gunsmith. "You let her into my room?"

"Mr. Adams, she wouldn't even argue with me. She said I better give her the key or else. And she also said you'd be mad at me if I didn't."

"And she also gave you some money."

The boy's face reddened. "Don't be mad at me, Mr. Adams. I've got to help an eighty-year-old mother."

The Gunsmith was halfway to the stairs. "Who said I was mad at you?"

The door was locked, but she must have heard him

coming down the corridor for it opened even as he gave the last rap.

"I thought you'd never get home."

"Better late than never."

She'd slipped back into bed, and he had only a flash of a silky white behind and a pair of marble white breasts that bounced as she ducked under the covers. She lay there with the sheet pulled up to her chin, her delightful eyes watching him as he undressed. As he came toward her she drew back the covers for him.

"I've been wanting you ever since . . . ever since ever," she said.

"Me too."

"Now you've got me."

"Now we've got each other." The Gunsmith corrected her as she directed his quivering organ into her yearning, wet bush.

When they'd finished she lay in his arms.

"My God, what a beautiful ending," Sally said. "It's like a wonderful book."

"This part," he said, reaching for her, "is only the beginning of the next chapter."